PATTON'S WALL

PATTON'S WALL

Leo Kessler

This first world edition published in Great Britain 1999 by
SEVERN HOUSE PUBLISHERS LTD of
9–15 High Street, Sutton, Surrey SM1 1DF.
This first world edition published in the U.S.A. 1999 by
SEVERN HOUSE PUBLISHERS INC of
595 Madison Avenue, New York, N.Y. 10022.

British Library Cataloguing in Publication Data

Kessler, Leo, 1926-
        Patton's wall
        1. Patton, George S. (George Smith), 1885-1945 - Fiction
        2. Eisenhower, Dwight D. (Dwight David), 1890-1969 - Fiction
        3. World War, 1939-1945 - Campaigns - Western Front - Fiction
        4. War stories
        I. Title
        823.9'14 [F]

        ISBN 0-7278-2261-6

All situations in this publication are fictitious and
any resemblance to living persons is purely coincidental.

Typeset by Palimpsest Book Production Ltd
Polmont, Stirlingshire, Scotland.
Printed and bound in Great Britain by
MPG Books Ltd, Bodmin, Cornwall.

THE PATTON PLOY

From here on in, it's either root-hog or die. Shoot the works. If those Hun bastards can do it that way, we can. If those sons of bitches want war in the raw, then that's the way we'll give it to 'em.

General Patton, December 1944

RENDEZVOUS WITH A GHOST

Old soldiers never die, they simply fade away.
First World War song.

B rigadier General Elmer D. Savage, US Army (retired) dressed himself with care. He always did although he was now old and very shaky – his frail, liver-spotted hands seemed to have a life of their own. Today was a special occasion, at least for him. Taking his time he pinned the rosettes of the Distinguished Service Cross and the Belgian *Croix de Guerre avec Palme* in the right lapel of his Brooks Brothers suit. Such things always pleased the Continentals.

Outside in Luxembourg's *Place de la Gare*, the morning traffic was building up already. The pre-nine o'clock rush of all the thousands of fat cats who worked in the capital's banks had commenced. Savage smiled carefully at himself in the mirror – he had to do so with care in order not to dislodge his false teeth, for his gums were receding again. "At seventy-six, old fellah," he said aloud in the fashion of lonely men, "you look everything else but savage." He dismissed the unpleasant thought and told himself wrily that when he had first seen that square below it had been under the fire of long-range German artillery from over the border and it had been jammed with truck after truck, all open in that freezing December cold, bearing reluctant heroes to the Third Army front just outside Bastogne up the road to the north.

He finished the rosettes, paused a moment to regain his breath and finished off by adjusting the Windsor knot; it helped to hide his scrawny, veined neck of which he was ashamed. Finally he set about pushing his thin, scraggy grey hair back and forth across his balding pate, trying to hide it. It was a vain old man's ritual, he told himself. It meant nothing. It wouldn't charm any of the well-dressed secretaries hurrying to their banks below; besides he hadn't had a woman for years now. "Holy cow," he said to himself, "what would *I* do with a woman now!"

Still, he thought, it *was* part and parcel of keeping up a front – like checking whether he smelled of piss like old men do and had shaved carefully at the side of his chin. And at his age 'front' was important. It was the last thing he had left before the funeral parlour. He sighed. He hoped that wouldn't be too long away; time seemed to drag interminably.

"Asshole," he snapped to his image in the mirror, with just a trace of that fire which had made him such a good combat soldier. "Have a butt and cheer your goddam self up." He looked at his hands. They were still trembling. He'd have to wait a few moments before they steadied sufficiently for him to work his old Zippo lighter. He smiled fondly. What would ole Hairless Harry have said, if he could see him and his hands now. "Jesus H., Savage," he'd have exclaimed. "What's wrong? – your mitts are doing a frigging jitterbug!" And then he'd remember he was speaking to his superior officer and he'd condescend to put a 'sir' on his comment. "Yeah, you're right there, Hairless," he said aloud again. "But then, old buddy, you've been dead over half a century now and you can't see just how far the 'old man' has gone down the frigging hill." "Amen to that, sir," Hairless agreed from the mirror, but Savage didn't seem to notice.

His bones creaking a little, he looked out of the window and up to the sky. No staff car from the military attaché yet, but the sky was leaden and threatening. It looked as if it might snow before the day was out. But then, he reminded himself, it always did in December in Lux. In all the years he had come here on what he called to himself 'my annual pilgrimage', it had always snowed. He would have missed it if it hadn't. After all, it had snowed and snowed that particular December, hadn't it?

Suddenly, in the way of old men he was fidgety and nervous, and didn't know why. He picked up the *Luxemburger Wort*, that national newspaper with its curious mix of German and French and even the local dialect – *Letzeburger* – often all three in the same column. Clinton was still in trouble, he saw. There was a picture of him, as usual full of piss and vinegar, that big schnoz of his sticking out of a hatchet face like a red *leberwurst*. He grinned maliciously. It couldn't be happening to a nicer guy. His Rangers, the survivors, that is, had booed the President when he had addressed them on the beaches six years before. "Draft dodger!" they jeered. Clinton hadn't turned a hair. Perhaps with all the crap on his head he wouldn't have been able to even if he had wanted to. He dismissed Clinton. He meant nothing to him. He was simply a part of an age that had no sense of duty and responsibility. 'Bullshitters' and 'Feather Merchants', his Rangers had called the type back when . . .

His mind wandered. He could see their long-dead faces as clearly as he had at Portsmouth that Monday morning, with the gale howling outside, when it had all started. 'Good ole boys', they called them today. They hadn't been 'good ole boys' at all. Hard, brutal young men of questionable morality – that's what they had been. But they had been patriots, prepared to die for their country. He sighed. Now where they had once died in their hundreds – thousands – there were these European fat cats hurrying to their plush banks, pudding faces full of greed, eager for another day of making money.

Abruptly he found himself crying softly and silently for no reason he could fathom. "Silly old fart", he cursed himself and dabbed his eyes in the same instant that the Portuguese maid tapped the door and said, "*Votre voiture vous attend.*" It was the

5

guy from the embassy. With a grunt, he raised himself from the chair, tipped the girl and went out into the December cold.

"So. I understand you do this every year, sir," the immaculately uniformed young captain of infantry from the embassy said, easing Savage out of the staff car and then, still holding him with one hand, giving him his stick.

Savage grunted something, too concerned with the business of standing upright again, hoping his left leg wouldn't begin its damned unpredictable trembling once again. The previous week in Germany where he had gone to view Hitler's 'Eagle's Nest' again, it had started trembling so much that he had pissed himself and hadn't noticed, till the bus driver, used to veterans, had pointed it out to him.

The captain was a typical West Pointer down to the outsize class ring and that 'sir' which he slapped onto every utterance he made. As old Hairless Harry would have snorted in disgust, 'Holy shit, Major that guy would land a 'sir' on one of my wet farts, honest Injun.'

"Yes," he answered finally. "I try . . . I'll keep it up as long as I can."

"I see, sir," the captain replied woodenly, though, of course, he didn't see. How could he?

Savage looked at the great portals to the military cemetery where three thousand of Patton's men had lain since 1945. It was deserted, save for a middle-aged Luxembourg civilian sweeping up the last of the fall leaves and glancing at his watch from time to time. Obviously he was checking when he could slip away for his morning *Bierpause* and a glance at the girls' tits in the German *Bildzeitung*. Naturally no one would miss him. It was winter. There were hardly any visitors in winter, though that was when most of them over there under those neat rows of white crosses had died.

"Would you like to see General Patton's grave first, General?" the captain enquired politely. He reached out to take Savage's frail arm.

Savage resisted the urge to pull away, as he knew he couldn't make it without assistance. "Yes, I guess I would," he answered politely. "Thank you, Captain."

"Be my guest, sir."

He would have liked to seen the graves of Hairless Harry and young 'Pissover' again, but he knew now he couldn't manage them even with assistance. He should have asked the embassy for a wheelchair, but he had been too proud. Now it was too late.

With the young captain's help, he hobbled towards Patton's grave, adorned with its simple three stars, his place of enlistment and his rank. He looked at the others, long lines of them bearing silent witness to the blood, the patriotism, self-sacrifice of another age. Next to him the captain thought something like that war would have been worth risking his neck for. It had all been a dramatic black and white with clear issues. For a moment he visualised the dead as he thought they might be: lean 'cool' youngsters, lounging a lot at street corners, eyeing the 'broads', as they would call them, garrison caps tilted down over their foreheads, smoking those forbidden cigarettes of theirs.

He forgot those GIs and their forbidden cigarettes and looked at the frail old general tottering at his side out of the corner of his eye. Naturally he knew all about him. At 'the Point' they had drilled that into them over and over again: always be well-briefed and then there can be no slip-ups. The general had been some sort of college prof. before Pearl Harbor. In '42 he'd enlisted in Intelligence, but had transferred to the new Rangers, based on the Brits' commandos. He'd fought right throughout the campaign to the Bulge when he had been attached to Patton's staff. Surprisingly enough the Army had kept him

7

on after the war when they'd been firing 'bird' colonels by the dozen. He'd gone through Korea and Vietnam and even managed to get himself wounded during the 'Tet' – and that was very rare for one-star generals. The word was he'd just missed the Congressional Medal of Honor because his mission in Vietnam had been too sensitive for public disclosure and no brigadier-general had won the CMH since D-Day. And now . . . involuntarily the captain shrugged . . . now he was just an old guy with death written all over him, whom you wouldn't have given a second look. Life was like that, he guessed, and suddenly he thrilled at the thought of Greta from the German embassy who spoke four languages and was so good in bed. Wow, it was wonderful to be young and not old.

"Patton." The old man stopped abruptly. "Bastard but a good soldier."

"You knew him personally, sir?"

"Yes. Funny . . ." the old man didn't really seem to hear his question" . . . no one ever seems to come to visit his grave save his old soldiers. Churchill was the last big shot to come up here – and that was back in '46."

The young captain forgot Greta of the four languages and cunning tongue. "Yeah, I've sometimes thought of that, sir, when we've been up on parade for Patton Day. President Eisenhower could have – he was in the area a lot in the '50s. Then there was President Bush and President Clinton back when he came to Bitburg just down the road." He ended, his handsome young face puckered in a puzzled frown.

The general looked up at his face, suddenly amused. It was that kind of half-malicious amusement that one sometimes sees on the faces of old men when they have managed to surprise young people. It says, 'You thought I was an ancient decrepit asshole, long past his sell-by date, didn't you? But I could tell you things you couldn't even dream about.' "Perhaps," he said, slowly and very deliberately, "the big shots, Ike, Bush, Clinton, etcetera knew something you didn't?"

"How do you mean sir?" the captain asked puzzled.

From Findel Airport just up the road an *Icelandic Air* plane took off with a thunderous roar just like the *Luftwaffe* bombers had done so long before. The captain waited patiently.

"About Patton," he indicated the grave with a stiff nod.

"Patton?"

"Yeah, Patton." The general coughed suddenly, deep and throaty. His frail body shook alarmingly. The captain gripped him hurriedly by the elbow, as if he might fall over at any moment. Choking a little, the general gasped. "You gotta a flask in the sedan?"

"Yessir. We always carry one – bourbon," the captain reddened as if he had admitted to some perverted inclination. "For an emergency," he added hurriedly. "It's standard operating procedure."

"'Kay, this *is* an emergency, son. Gimme a slug . . . and . . . and I'll tell you a tale you'll be able to dine out on for the rest of your born days. Come on, I need that drink . . ."

PART I

Just give me the gas, and I'll go through the Siegfried Line like shit through a goose!

General Patton, Fall 1944

One

THIS IS YOUR ROAD TO THE REICH, the mud-splattered, stencilled sign read COURTESY 8 US COMBAT ENGINEERS. Col. Eugene Peabody Commanding.

The officer in the lead jeep nudged his driver. The soldier in the camouflaged smock, bare of badges of rank or unit identity, stopped. But he kept the engine running. Its exhaust fogged the icy Lorraine air. As the officer stood up to study the scene, the second jeep bumping down the muddy trail out of the shattered pine forest came to a halt too. Its driver kept his engine running as well.

If the muddy village street, along which the tail-to-tail convoy of US Sherman tanks crawled, was really heading for the Reich, twenty miles away, it seemed as if it was going to be an awfully long journey. Everywhere there were signs that the US Third Army's assault on the German border fortresses was running into trouble – serious trouble.

In the shell-pitted fields further on, there were dead cows everywhere. They lay on their sides, bodies bloating and stinking, legs protruding rigidly up like so many tethered barrage balloons. They weren't alone. There was a big tank destroyer, one track stretched out behind it like a broken limb. Not far away there was a box-like ambulance, window shattered, all four tyres burst, the wounded it had been carrying sprawled grotesquely in the muddy grass, dead. Next to them a bunch of frightened blacks of the Graves Registration Commission rested on their shovels, as they dug the graves for the dead, talking among themselves in hushed tones.

The officer standing in the front of the first jeep knew the signs. He had seen it all before – too often! These Yanks were going nowhere. He flashed a look in the direction of the front. Over the grim sinister heights which were the Reich, the guns had commenced once more – the exploding shells flickering a silent pink. Patton's Third Army was attacking again and they were getting nowhere. The defenders would hold them as they had been doing for the last six weeks. A salvo of shells on this God-forsaken Lorraine 'cow village' and the Yanks would be running for their lives again, throwing away their weapons in their unreasoning panic.

He spat drily into the mud and grunted something to the driver. The latter moved swiftly. He knew the danger they were in – they all did. It wasn't wise to stay around anywhere too long if they wanted to live. He thrust home the gear and let out the clutch. They started to move through the thick clinging mud. Behind them the driver of the second jeep did the same. Next to him, the man in the camouflaged smock without badges clutched his Sten gun more tightly, as if there might be trouble at any moment.

They edged their way onto the village street and started dodging in and out of the almost stationary tanks. Their drivers didn't object as they might have done normally. It was obvious to the officer in the first jeep that the Yankee drivers were only too glad to stay where they were. They were in no hurry to get on the 'road to the Reich' . . . 'courtesy of the 8th Combat Engineers', whoever in hell's name they were.

At a snail's pace, the little convoy passed a battery of what appeared to be abandoned field howitzers. Around each cannon there was a pile of shells, neatly arranged and, here and there, covered with a tarpaulin to keep off the persistent snow-rain of this desolate part of Northern France. But their crews were nowhere in sight.

The officer sniffed. Typical, he told himself and then flashed a look at the two GIs in long black slickers, squatting in a ditch next to an anti-tank gun. Their faces were pale, bearded and lost. They didn't look up as the two jeeps trundled by.

They turned a corner. The sound of the gunfire from the front was getting louder. Here and there the men in the jeeps could see the signal flares sailing urgently into the leaden sky. The Yanks were in trouble, obviously. They were demanding help. The officer in the lead jeep rubbed his well-shaven chin. One might well have thought he seemed pleased at the sight.

A typical Lorraine village square. The public washhouse in the centre, a couple of shabby estaminets advertising "Mousel"; the *mairie*, with a shabby, frayed *tricolour* flag hanging down limply at its doorless entrance. Everywhere there were American infantry. They squatted on their grey haunches in the mud, heads sunk between their knees in defeat. Others stood around a fire made of window frames and doors ripped from the houses around the square, warming their chapped, brick-red hands. Officers paced back and forth nervously, discussing the situation in low anxious voices. Occasionally they flashed covert glances at their dispirited men.

A younger officer, with his officer's bars removed, as if he were afraid there might be German snipers up in the roofs of the abandoned houses, staggered up to the jeeps. He was drunk. They could smell the bourbon on his breath even at that distance. "The big frigging bugout," he announced apropos of nothing and swayed. "Jesus H. Christ, what a mess!"

The officer in the lead jeep said nothing. But a keen observer might have noticed that his right hand had slid almost automatically to his pistol holster. "That frigging feather-merchant Patton," the American went on, not seeing the gesture "frigging old blood and guts Patton – Yeah," his

15

dirty, worn face contorted bitterly. *"Our* frigging blood and *his* frigging guts!"

If he had expected any reaction, he was disappointed.

The officer stared down at him stonily as if he were some strange creature from another planet.

The American was perhaps too drunk to notice. He said, "You guys going forward?" Suddenly he stopped and, focusing his eyes as best he could, he said, "But you guys are limeys, ain't ya?" He stared at the hard-faced men in the two jeeps in bewilderment. "What the Sam Hill are you doing in this goddam neck o' the wood, eh?"

"Special troops," the man in the jeep answered hastily. Next to him, the driver pressed his foot down harder on the gas pedal. Obviously he wanted to be off. The officer next to him flashed him a warning look. "Yes," he said in careful British English, as if he half expected that the other man would have difficulty in understanding him, "We're on a special mission from Nancy." He meant the US Third Army's HQ.

"Gee, *Nancy*," the US officer breathed the word, as if he had just mentioned paradise. "Beer, bed and babes. Oh brother! What wouldn't yours truly give to go to Nancy just now. It would be worth losing my right nut for—" He broke off suddenly, as an angry shout was followed a moment later by the sharp crack of a single rifle shot like a dry twig snapping underfoot in a summer forest. He swung round.

To his right, a drunken GI had staggered out of one of the two estaminets, clutching his left arm. Bright red blood was seeping through his dirty fingers as he held them to his new wound, crying, "The sonuvabitch just plugged me – the crazy bastard! . . . Just went and shot me—"

A fat woman followed the shot man out. Her blouse had been ripped open at the front to reveal her monstrous breasts shimmying back and forth like puddings as she moved. She waved angrily at the GI and cried, *"Salaud . . . sale con americain*—" Then she saw the American officer staring at her. She reacted immediately. Swinging round swiftly for one so fat, the blonde lifted up her skirts to reveal her great naked flanks – and the fact, too, that she wasn't a true blonde – crying, *"Merde . . . merde—"*

The drunken officer's mouth dropped open at the sight of that tremendous amount of naked dimpled flesh and for a moment he forgot these strange Englishmen in their midst. The officer in the jeep didn't give him chance to recover. He nudged the driver with his elbow sharply. The man didn't need any urging. He pressed home the gas pedal. The jeep shot forward, followed instantly by the other. In a matter of moments they had vanished into the mess of stalled armour and by the time the officer had realised it there was little he could do. So he stood there, while the woman ranted and the wounded GI bemoaned his fate, muttering to himself, "What's them limeys doing here in the middle of a goddam shooting war? They should be in old London town, sitting comfy-like on their skinny limey keesters, drinking frigging China tea . . ."

Five minutes later the strangers were doing something more drastic than sitting 'comfy-like' on their 'skinny limey keesters' drinking 'frigging China tea'. They had swung out of the last of the houses bordering the littered road heading to the front and were about to turn south-west away from the fighting, when it happened. Suddenly, startlingly, the boy stepped into the road, grease gun in one hand, the other raised: a boy in uniform. Still, there was determination written all over his unlined youthful features. *"Halt,"* he commanded in a thin voice, as the first jeep slithered to an abrupt stop on the mud-slick road. As if to emphasise his command, he raised the evil-looking machine pistol he carried slung from his skinny shoulder. Behind the leading jeep the driver of the second one cursed furiously, as he attempted to brake without sliding into it.

17

For a moment or two the big tough men in their camouflaged smocks and red berets wearing the strange blue winged dagger badge on their headgear were caught completely off guard by the sudden challenge out of nowhere.

The boy standing at the side of the road appeared not to notice. His earnest skinny face beneath the overlarge helmet displayed only purpose; after all it was his duty to check and identify any vehicle leaving the village by this side road. *"ID?"* he called in a ready voice, his prominent Adam's apple racing up and down his skinny throat like an express elevator. "Let's see some ID, driver." He jerked up the muzzle of his grease gun as if to emphasise the command.

A little helplessly the driver of the jeep looked at the officer at his side. He nodded slightly. The driver started to fumble with his smock pocket. The sentry watched him all the time, as if he was telling himself that he knew it was merely a drill; but that all the same, the correct procedure had to be adhered to.

The officer in the camouflaged uniform didn't take his gaze off the boy's serious face for one instant. But beneath the cover of the windshield, his right hand fumbled with the shaft in his high boot. Suddenly his heart was beating crazily. He didn't know why. He had done this often enough before – and the sentry was only a raw kid, still wet behind the ears. He guessed he'd never get used to killing his fellow human beings.

The boy grew impatient while the driver continued to fumble, knowing as he did so that the identification they had been provided with temporarily wouldn't hold up. In a minute the kid would be asking for the day's password and then they'd really be up to their hooters in shit. Naturally he didn't have it. Sweating in spite of the bone-chilling arctic wind that seemed to be blowing straight from Siberia, he prayed fervently that X would act – *soon.*

"C'm on," the boy urged impatiently, stamping his frozen

feet, his overshoes heavy with mud. "Cripes, this cold is freezing up my—" He never finished his little lament.

A flash of silver. A cry of alarm, stifled deep down in the kid's throat. The grease gun tumbled from the sentry's suddenly nerveless fingers. He sank to his knee in the mud almost immediately as if he were praying to some God above him for mercy. But God was looking the other way this cold brutal December day.

With his booted foot the driver lashed out viciously. The boot caught the dying boy in his contorted face. His helmet flew off to reveal a long lock of blond hair that fell over his forehead. He slammed down into the grey goo. Strange terrible noises came from deep down inside his skinny throat.

Without waiting for an order. A man in the back of the jeep vaulted over the side like a trained athlete. He ripped the knife out of the dying boy's chest with an obscene sucking noise. For an instant the blade gleamed red against the silver. Next moment the man plunged the knife home again. Red gore spurted up and drenched the man's clenched fist holding the killing blade. The boy's spine curved in a tight bow momentarily. Then he gave a strange little gasp. He fell back into the mud. Mouth gaping stupidly like that of some village idiot, his head with that lock of bright yellow hair flopped to one side. He was dead.

The officer nodded his approval. Gasping a little, the killer lifted up the dead boy as if he weighed no more than a small child. Ignoring the blood dripping down on his knees, he half-doubled to the skeletal winter bushes a dozen yards away from the road. With a grunt he tossed the boy into them, as if he were getting rid of a sack of rubbish. At the jeeps the drivers were gunning their engines once more impatiently. Thick grey fumes formed on the icy air. The man got the message. He ran full-tilt to the first jeep. Already it was beginning to move off, as he threw himself over the side.

19

Next to the driver, clutching the jeep's windscreen as he steadied himself, the officer in the red beret flashed one last look at the scene of the murder. Apparently he thought everything was all right, for he turned to the second jeep and yelled above the noise of the engines, *"Los vorwärts, Kurt . . . dalli . . . dalli, Mensch!"*

Moments later the little convoy had vanished down the D road which led away from the Reich to the west. In the bush, the body of the murdered boy had already begun to stiffen in that freezing cold . . .

Two

With their sirens screeching the little procession of scout cars, filled with heavily armed MPs, roared at full speed through Nancy's *Place Stanislas*. Behind came the big open olive-drab Packard, bearing the three silver stars of a lieutenant-general on its hood. Standing upright in the back of the Packard, as if he were some Roman emperor in his ornamental chariot, the commander of the US Third Army stared imperiously at the shabby French civilians who lined the route, despite the freezing cold. The women in their old-fashioned regional bonnets curtsied and the old men with the ribbons of the Old War on their shabby jacket lapels whipped off their navy-blue berets hastily, as if they might well be in trouble from this foreign general, who had appeared so suddenly in their midst two months before, if they didn't.

But the scowl on the general's stern face underneath the gleaming lacquered helmet with its outsize three silver stars didn't relax. He was practising his 'war face, number three' and when he wore his 'war-face', he never smiled in that sinister threatening manner of his – his only concession to warmth and humour.

At top speed, well above the thirty-kilometre-an-hour speed limit, the convoy swept down the *Rue du Sergent Blandau*; the over-aged gendarmes, togged out in white gloves for the morning procession, saluted smartly. Still the general didn't appear to notice. Perhaps, they told themselves as the shrieking

21

convoy streaked past splashing them with the fresh slush-snow which had fallen on the capital of Lorraine overnight, he had overdone it with one of those American mistresses of his the previous night.

But on this cold morning with a hint of fresh snow in the leaden sky, the Army Commander had other thoughts on his mind than the nubile bodies of naked USO canteen girls. The front was worrying him. For nearly two months now he had been promising 'Ike' – the Supreme Commander, General Eisenhower in Paris – that he would go through the 'Krauts' in Lorraine like 'shit through a goose'. But he had still to realise that boast. The German fortress at Metz, the key to the route to Nazi Germany, was holding out against everything he could throw at the damned place. Soon the winter would set in in all its dreaded fury in this goddam arsehole of the world in Lorraine and all major offensive operations would perforce come to an end. This day he would fly to Metz and kick ass. He had to get the op. on the goddam road before it was too late.

Five minutes later the convoy was slowing down. The MPs started to relax. They had gotten the 'Old Man' safely to his HQ once more. Now they could put up their big feet and simmer down over a cup of steaming hot 'Java'. With luck somebody might be tooting an illicit bottle of French cognac and they'd get a slug of the frog hooch as well.

The lead scout car turned into the former French *caserne*. The sentries, as polished and as smart as if they were still on garrison duty back stateside, clicked to attention and presented arms. The commanding general gave them the works. He brought his elegantly gloved hand to the brim of his gleaming helmet and saluted them with all the precision of the West Point cadet that he had once been so many years ago. He obviously was pleased with the sentries" turnout for he even gave them the benefit of his dingy-toothed smile.

Then they were slowing down, with the MPs springing out of their vehicles, tommy-guns at the ready to form a defensive circle around the commanding general's sedan and from the open door of the main building, the brass, all 'pinks', elegant tunics and gleaming polished riding boots, came streaming out smiling hugely to welcome the Old Man.

Patton was used to their fawning attentions. Indeed he welcomed them. They made him feel secure, in charge, the master of the situation, the all-knowing, all-powerful boss man. As they ushered him inside 'out of the cold, General' they grovelled and asked how he'd slept, whether he had been disturbed the previous night by the 'impertinence' of a 'Kraut hit-and-run raider' over Nancy. A full bird colonel asked permission to light his big Cuban cigar. He nodded his approval. Another gently removed his expensive gabardine raincoat. A third took his lacquered helmet as if it were a very precious gift. Then he was inside, striding across the squeaking polished floor towards the big echoing map room.

Colonel Koch, his chief of intelligence, was waiting for him, pointer already clutched in his hand. Koch was a 'kike', but he was as smart as a whip and Patton needed him. Behind the bespectacled intelligence man, his two corps commanders, Gerow and Eddy waited to report and accept his orders. They both looked ill at ease. He knew why but for the moment he concentrated his full attention on Koch.

"General Patton," Koch said, using the army commander's name to display the intimacy that existed between him, a lowly colonel, and the three-star general. Patton smiled carefully to himself. The Kike was a very smart operator, he noted. "Yes, Koch," he said, puffing an idle smoke ring. "You can begin."

Koch tapped the huge map of the western front with his pointer like the schoolmaster he had once been. An immediate silence fell on the big room. The morning briefing could commence . . .

"So," Koch summed up half an hour later, feeling a little drained at trying to remember so many details of units, terrain, supplies, casualties – a hundred and one items – without reference to his notes, "you can see gentlemen, the Krauts have – if you'll excuse my French," he looked at Patton, who was the most profane man in the whole of the Third Army – "gotten us by the short and curlies. We've tried to attack round them on the left flank." He shrugged his plump shoulders. "No deal." We've tried the right flank. Same result, only more casualties. In essence," he ended, not drawing any conclusions for that was not his business, "the Krauts know our every move. Half the population of the area are German-speaking and pro-Kraut and the enemy has got his spies everywhere. The only solution would be to clear out the whole of the civvie population," he shrugged again, "and General de Gaulle's provisional government in Paris wouldn't like that, I guess."

"Frigging Krauts." Patton took his cigar out of his mouth and exclaimed routinely and without rancour. *"Worse – frigging Frogs!"*

Koch didn't react. He had done his bit. His job was finished for this morning.

Patton didn't ask him any questions. He said softly, "Thank you, Koch. Fine exposé."

Slowly he turned to his two corps commanders while the rest of the staff tensed. This was always the worst moment of the morning briefing. It was when General Patton made up his mind and gave out his orders. More generals had died a sudden death at this point than ever did on a battlefield. They waited . . .

Patton didn't pull his punches, "Gentlemen," he announced solemnly, "we will attack Fort Driant once more tomorrow morning. I have made my decision." He paused and added, "I know . . . I know, we've done it before, the weather's lousy and Lorraine is full of Kraut agents, the bastards! But you never know what might happen to the – er – gentlemen up north." He meant his rival US army commanders in the Belgian Ardennes to the north of Lorraine. "They might well be screaming frigging blue murder soon, and that would be the end of the Third Army's drive into the Reich. Naturally Mrs Patton's handsome son is not going to allow that, no siree!"

If the Third Army Commander thought his sortie would amuse his two corps commanders he was mistaken. General Eddy, round-faced, bespectacled, continued to look worried, very worried. "But General," he objected, "you can't expect my corps to attack Fort Driant in these conditions. Air support would be nil – and my divisions are very tired, sir."

Patton's wintry smile vanished. He looked severely at his XII Corps Commander, "There are no tired divisions, General," he snapped, "only tired commanders."

"That may be, General," Eddy persisted, his fat face growing redder still. He was attempting to conceal his dangerously high blood pressure, but he knew he was showing every sign of the condition at this moment. "But conditions in the field are hell for my kids. Trenchfoot and chest colds are endemic up there."

"They ain't *kids* and their complaints are due to poor supervision by their troop officers," Patton warned.

But his senior officers didn't heed the warning in Patton's thin voice. Grow, the commander of Eddy's 6th Armored Division, said hotly, "Sir, I agree with General Eddy. Another attack would be simply throwing away valuable American lives."

Patton gave the two officers the benefit of his frightening 'Number One Frown' while the staff waited for the explosion soon to come. None came. Instead Patton asked quietly, "You feel that under the present conditions, you cannot undertake the attack as I intend?"

"That is correct," they answered promptly and in unison.

Patton didn't hesitate. He said calmly, "Then would you prefer to make recommendations as to your successors, gentlemen?"

Just behind the commanding general, Colonel Charles Codman, his senior aide, told himself, 'Here we go. The shit's hit the fan.' All around him the top brass froze. A heavy tense silence descended upon the big room. Outside a petulant voice was saying, "If I say you'll fill in that form blank in triplicate, that's exactly what you'll do. In triplicate. Do you understand?"

Then Patton spoke again. The menace had vanished from his voice now. Instead it was full of warmth and encouragement, as he said, "Please come on over to the map and I'll tell you exactly what I want you to do."

Codman breathed a sigh of relief. The crisis was over.

Now for twenty minutes Patton lectured his reluctant generals, pumping their drained reservoirs of confidence full of his own elixir of vitality and determination. "So you see, gentlemen," he urged finally, "the problem of Driant isn't as insurmountable as you thought. Major Savage's Rangers are going to draw the Krauts" teeth first by knocking out the covering batteries. After that it will be a comparative walkover for your GI Joes . . ."

'*Savage*,' Codman intoned the familiar, if somewhat frightening name of the Ranger leader to himself. One very tough nut, he told himself. As ruthless as the Old Man, but smarter and very much more devious. He didn't wear his heart – if he had one – on his sleeve like Patton did. All the same, if anyone could do it and finally put an end to the bloody mess at Metz it would be Savage and his bunch of intellectual thugs . . .

Patton took his gaze off the war-torn countryside below and sighed. Colonel Codman, a former pilot himself, who had been watching both the terrain and the cocky young pilot, who didn't look a day over eighteen, turned his attention immediately to his boss. It wasn't often that 'Ole Blood an' Guts' sighed – he wasn't the sighing kind of general. "Everything all right, sir?" he asked, while an anxious little voice at the back of his mind hissed, I hope that dumb cluck of a so-called pilot realises that we have only five minutes" flying time left before we hit Kraut territory.

Patton sighed again. At that moment he looked every day of his fifty-nine years of age. "You know, Charley," he said slowly, as the ground sped beneath them and they could see the first slit trench lines – abandoned – which indicated they were getting very close to Metz, "I think this has been the longest goddam day of the war for me."

"Sir." Codman nodded his understanding. The General's mood was now as damp and depressed as this cold winter's morning. Soon it was going to snow, too; that wouldn't make things any easier at the front. Brother, the little voice inside whined, when will this goddam war ever come to an end. It seemed to have been going on for an eternity. "I can believe that, sir," he heard himself saying. "But there are better times ahead, sir, I'm sure." He tried to cheer his boss.

Patton didn't look at him, suddenly he was staring at something to their front. "Do you think, so, Charley?" he asked absently. "At this moment, I feel lower than a whale's ass – say, what do you make of that!" There was abrupt urgency in his voice.

"What?"

"There at three o'clock high."

Codman craned his neck, as up front the young pilot, the earphones crushing his garrison cap to the back of his crew-cut head, stopped chewing gum and looked worried – or as worried as his kind of youth ever could be, Codman told himself.

A dark shape was hurtling out of the grey leaden sky

27

straight at the little unarmed spotter plane, zapping through the intermittent cloud at a tremendous rate.

"Kraut?" Patton asked quickly, voice devoid of fear.

"No sir," Codman tried to reassure his boss, at the same time trying to identify the shape of the unknown plane – a fighter obviously – from the recognition charts he had studied so long ago. "But what it is other than a Messerschmitt I don't kn—" The words died on his lips.

Suddenly – startlingly – white tracer was converging on the little plane at a tremendous rate. "Holy cow!" the young pilot yelled, "they're frigging well firing at us." Next instant he had jerked up the joystick and the plane shot straight upwards and for a horrifying moment seemed to be suspended in mid-air by its prop.

"You stupid . . ." Codman's words of protest were drowned by the unknown fighter flashing by them, narrowly missing a collision at four hundred miles an hour. The colonel caught a fleeting glimpse of the red, white and blue of the RAF and then the Spitfire was surging upwards, dragging a sudden white contrail behind it and he was gasping to Patton, "It's one of ours, sir . . . a Royal Air Force Spitfire!"

Patton was unimpressed. "Well, if it's a limey that goddam pilot badly needs his eyes testing – *Shit*, Codman, the crazy bastard's coming in again!"

Codman felt sudden fear. Patton was right. The Spitfire pilot had executed a skilful tight turn – only an expert pilot could do that – had righted himself and was coming in for another attack. This time he had lowered his undercarriage to reduce his speed so that he could get a better aim. In a flash Codman realised that this wasn't a mistake; that guy in the Spit, was out to shoot them out of the sky *deliberately*! "TAKE EVASIVE ACTION, YOU STUPID MORON!" he yelled frantically at the pilot over the racket. "NOW – THAT GUY'S OUT TO MURDER US!"

The kid at the controls seemed to wake up out of a daze. He jerked the plane to the right and then went into a steep dive. Patton nodded his approval, but his stern face showed no fear. Codman"s, in contrast, revealed all his doubts, as the L-5 dived. But now he could see the kid knew his business. He was beginning to hedge-hop, flying at almost zero feet, changing course every couple of seconds, trying to put their unknown enemy off his shot. Fervently praying like he had never done since he had left grade school, the hook-nosed, upper-crust colonel from Boston hoped he was going to pull it off.

A stream of tracer zipped lethally past their cockpit canopy. It beat the skeletal hedgerow to their right. White-split twigs and red berries flew everywhere. A flock of birds rose in hoarse protest. Narrowly the Spitfire pilot avoided them. But he wasn't put off by his close escape. He persisted with his daring attack, obviously knowing that he had only to make the slightest error of judgement and he would be ploughing into the earth without a chance of survival.

Patton tugged at his ivory-handled pistol in his right holster. "I'm gonna get the bastard personally," he blustered, red-faced with sudden rage. "Who the hell does that guy think he is—"

"General, general," Codman grabbed his hand to restrain him in the same moment that a vicious salvo of slugs ripped the length of the fuselage and flooded the interior with icy air. Up front the young pilot was bleeding from a sudden wound in his left shoulder. But he didn't let go of the controls for one moment. He stuck to them as if his very life depended upon it – which it did.

The Spitfire pilot slowed down now to just above stalling speed. Codman tensed. This was the moment of truth, he knew it from his own combat flying days. He felt the sweat begin to trickle unpleasantly down the small of his back. He started to count off the seconds till the Spitfire pilot would open fire.

Three . . . four . . . The Spitfire filled the whole sky behind them. Codman stared at it transfixed. He could make out the plane's every rivet now. It wouldn't be long. Abruptly, long violent lights crackled the length of the Spitfire's wings. This was it . . .

Three

They split up in front of the eighteenth-century *caserne*, built by Vauban for his master, the Sun King, when France ruled Europe. Now the French were everyone's dogs bodies, Savage told himself, and it was America, which would soon dominate Europe – and the rest of the world, too, for that matter. Even the *caserne*, once an outpost on the Bourbons" new empire was occupied by a black GI supply company, working the 'Red Ball Express' route.*

Major Savage, once associate professor of European History at College Park, Maryland, forgot eighteenth-century French expansionism and concentrated on the task in hand. Followed by an apparently casual group of his Rangers, hands in their pockets, caps on the backs of their heads, as if they were out on the razzle, enjoying a few hours out of the mayhem of war, he strolled across the cobbled square in front of the black supply company's base.

A shaft of yellow light slit the blackout. Momentarily he could hear the thick throaty chuckles of drunken black marketeers, and the cheap shrill laughter of their whores. In the background there was the tinny accordion music of a

---

* Supply route right from the Normandy beaches to the fighting front, crossing France and Belgium and into Germany: one road up and one road down. Traffic discipline enforced by US military policemen, who had orders to shoot at any infringement.

bal musette band playing a *java*. Savage could just imagine the frogs dancing belly-to-belly in the jerky rhythm with the women thrusting their hands into the pockets of their partners playing with their balls. He sighed and told himself nobody would be playing with his balls this cold winter's night – more the pity. As the door closed he gazed at the vanishing yellow light enviously. *Quel dommage!*

He and the others turned casually into the hilltop town's main street. There was a line of blacks lined up outside the green-lighted pro-station. They'd been with the whores; now as regulations stipulated they would have to receive their anti-VD treatment at the station; if they didn't and got the clap, they'd be for the stockade. The supreme commander had made VD a punishable offence in the US Army.

A crowd of GIs, whites this time, came swaggering up the street. The chatter of the blacks ceased. They slunk into the shadows – 'invisible men,' Savage told himself, in a segregated Army that only used them as cooks, clerks, drivers: second class citizens, the lot of them.

The GIs were in a bad mood. Savage could hear that more than see it in the blacked-out gloom. They swore at the 'niggers', shouted at a fat French woman hurrying past that she'd better watch out, 'cos them niggers ain't really human. They've got tails like chimps and they live off coconuts and Frog flesh.' That occasioned a great laugh and they staggered on, now singing drunkenly, "We're the boys of the ole seventy-ninth, we'd rather fuck than fight" to disappear into the night: cannon fodder, the poor bloody infantry, getting drunk and getting laid before they went back to that brutal killing machine at Metz to suffer the inevitable fate.

All the same he was glad he and his men hadn't bumped into the poor bastards. There would have been a fight. Everyone attempted to take a sock at the Rangers to show just tough they were, boasting afterwards they had 'mixed it' with the élite of the US Army, not mentioning naturally that they had been put on their backs in a matter of minutes in most cases.

Savage smiled warily in the darkness and noticed that 'Hairless Harry', his totally bald bodyguard, had edged a little closer to the 'boss' in case the drunken GIs had attempted to start something.

Savage forgot the drunken GIs and concentrated on his problem. General Patton had given him one hell of a task, especially here in Lorraine. The eastern province was riddled with informers, 'left-behind agents' and 'collabos', who were still working for the Krauts. In part it was due to the fact that a sizeable number of the locals were German-speakers and thought themselves still German. Then there was the problem of those supposed French patriots and their like all over Europe who had been on a good thing with the enemy.

Back in the States in the early '40s, he had readily accepted Hollywood's version of occupied Europe, full of brave men and women fighting their German occupiers (usually sadistic swine in the black uniform of the SS) with every weapon at their disposal and bravely dying for the 'Resistance' if necessary (naturally in a suitably heroic manner and at some length).

The reality had been totally different. When he and his Rangers had come ashore on D-Day they had been stopped dead by Hitler's Atlantic Wall. But the men who had built that wall had been mainly Frenchmen and the weapons they had used to slaughter the 'Big Red One'* on Omaha Beach had been manufactured by that same 'oppressed, occupied' nation and half a dozen similar European peoples. From the French-constructed bunkers, with the steel cupolas manufactured by Renault, they had mown down the GI attackers on the beach below with Czech Skoda cannon and Belgian manufactured machine guns.

* The 1st US Infantry Division.

It was then Savage had begun to realise that the great mass of occupied Europe just wanted to be left alone to get on with its own affairs; while a sizeable minority had actively supported their conquerors. Then, after being shot at by French women snipers in German pay, attacked by Belgian and Dutch SS formations and having their vehicles sabotaged by renegade Indians who had joined the 'Indian Legion', he had come to trust no one in Europe.

Now his intention was to lay a false trail. For he knew that his special Ranger Long Range Penetration Force was well known to the smartasses of German Intelligence and their paid helpers in the local civilian population; he had to be very careful. If he wasn't, he and his men would find themselves up in front of an enemy firing squad one fine morning – and that was something that ex-Associate Professor, Dr Stephen Savage, of the University of Maryland, founded 1806, was working assiduously to avoid.

"You wanna fuck?" the brittle female voice asked in crude GI English. "Sucki sucki, ficki ficki – anyway you like GI." He turned round startled, College Park, the University of Maryland, forgotten immediately.

A whore was standing in the bullet-pocked doorway of the house to his left, a torch pressed lightly to the soft bulge of her skinny belly suggestively, the blue light illuminating her sharp, venal face.

She looked like all the other whores in that street: long, shoulder-length hair, too young for her prematurely aged features; shaggy hip-length rabbit-fur jacket; thin flowered dress with no slip beneath – and no panties either. He could see that clearly even in the light of the blacked-out torch. "You want it, GI?" she asked with professional concupiscence, her thick-lipped, red mouth opened, tip of her tongue protruding suggestively.

"Five buck, American for single jump. Ten for night. I kiss,

GI. French kiss love." She ran her tongue round her slack wet lips to make her meaning quite clear.

Behind her one of the GI drunks had a black on the floor and was kicking him brutally, as he lay curled up, not attempting to defend himself, just trying to cover his face. The whore came closer. Still holding the lit torch, she reached out and squeezed his penis. She did so in a routine, manner like some peasant woman feeling a piece of fruit to check whether it was ripe enough. Behind him Hairless Harry made a tut-tutting sound. Savage pulled a face. The episode would be round the whole troop before morning. "Five dollars, American . . . nice hand job," she began, voice artificially warm and cajoling. She stopped abruptly and when she spoke again, her tone had changed immediately, her 'business' forgotten now. "You Ranger?" she hissed, looking to left and right as if Hitler himself might be listening to her.

He nodded, wondering if he was right and whether he had finally made contact with the man he had come to see in this God forsaken fortress in the middle of the wilds of Lorraine.

"Whitey told us to look for you-all, girls look Ranger," she hissed.

His heart skipped a beat. *He'd touched down!* "Whitey, you said?" he snapped hurriedly.

She nodded in a conspiratorial fashion. Like all whores she enjoyed secrets and plots. Perhaps it was an antidote to the boring life of spreading her legs every couple of hours or so. Gossip had to be a real change from lying on your back, staring morosely at some peeling ceiling, while a sweaty, smelly, grunting man pumped himself up and down on top of you, as if his very life depended upon it.

"What do you know about Whitey?" he whispered urgently, signalling with his hand behind his back for Hairless Hairy to come closer. Tangling with the mysterious Whitey, deserter

35

Leo Kessler

and alleged King Rat of the Red Ball Express, was supposed to be a very dangerous business indeed.

"All right, you know enough," the whore said testily, as if she, too, had suddenly realised it could be dangerous to talk too much about Whitey. "You want him?"

"Yes," Savage answered. On the pavement behind him in the darkness the drunken white GI was thudding his boot routinely into the prostrate black's ribs grunting, "That'll larn ya, not to interfere with our white women, you coloured trash."

Under other circumstances, Savage would have found the remark sourly ludicrous – 'our white women'! But not now. The new mission was too important to let himself be deflected from the main purpose.

"You will lead me to him – this Whitey?" he asked.

"Yes, *bien sûr*," she answered promptly and for once she didn't ask for 'dollars American' for the service; he felt that was significant.

She left them in a smoke-filled bar at the far end of the town. It was packed with GIs, most drunk, and whores, also drunk, but still able to add up and make ten dollars out of five. Savage sat over his weak wartime beer. In the flyblown, cracked mirror behind it, he could see Hairless Harry positioned next to the thick felt blackout blanket at the door, one hand dug deep into the pocket of his 'Ike Jacket', where he kept the little captured German Walther 7.62mm pistol. He smiled happily. Old Hairless never relaxed his vigilance for a moment.

Behind the bar, the runt of a barman, *Gauloise* glued to his bottom, lip – "Nix Frog here. We speak only GI American," he had announced sourly when Savage had ordered his beer in French – put down a glass on the zinc counter awash with suds and said, "Whitey, he see you now." He jerked his head towards the door next to the one which led to the urine-stench of the *cour*. "No waste time, savvy?"

36

"Savvy". Savage put down his glass hurriedly, half full.

Behind him Hairless Harry licked his lips greedily. He could have sunk the rest of that weak frog piss without any pain. But there was no time for that. With seeming casualness, he eased his way through the noisy drunken throng after his boss.

Savage paused in front of the door. His Colt .45 was in the leather holster at his side. But he felt he'"d need his back-up at the ready – just in case. He felt into the hole in his right pocket, tugged the string to which his second little pistol was attached. He pulled it closer to the hole, ready for a quick draw, knocked and without waiting for an answer, went in.

The room was empty save for the man sitting at the bare table, but he caught the whiff of some expensive fragance or other and guessed there had been a woman in the place only moments before. The man looked up, gravely and in straight English, without a trace of the usual negro inflection, he said politely, "Please take a seat Major Savage. I've been expecting you. Perhaps we'll discuss business first and then have a drink afterwards. That's if a Southern gentleman from the state of Maryland will drink at the same table as a nigrah." The sting in the tail hit home.

Savage wasn't offended. He had already learned one thing from it: Whitey had been looking into his background, just as he had into the black man's. Airily he said, "Not at all, Lieutenant White. I'd deem it a minor honour." He emphasised the 'minor'.

Whitey grinned, showing those perfect teeth of his, "*Touché*, Major," he said.

Savage looked at the handsome black for a moment. The man would have been the ideal subject for a US Army recruiting poster – hard jaw, lean handsome face, keen piercing eyes, which radiated leadership and determination. There was only one thing wrong with it – the face was black, coal black!

Despite the deserter's name there was nothing of the 'high yaller' about him. He was one hundred per cent of negro descent.

Whitey's grin vanished. He was hard and very businesslike now. "Let's talk turkey, Major," he snapped. "You haven't ventured into this particular den of iniquity to exchange pleasantries. I know that. But," he leaned forward urgently, "before you tell me I'll tell you what I want in return."

Savage was impressed by the deserter's bluntness. Whitey knew that Savage could summon up a whole battalion of MPs to capture him, if he wished, though it would be a tough assignment. The authorities had tried before, but Whitey had always been warned in time – after all every black in the ETO* admired him. Yet here he was laying down conditions. Either the man was a fool, which Savage didn't think he was for one single moment, or he had a brass neck of massive proportions. "What?"

"Just that General Eisenhower's boys keep off my back for the next four weeks."

Savage was puzzled. "Why the next four weeks?"

Now it was Whitey's turn to look puzzled too. "I can't put my finger on it exactly, Major," he said a little hesitantly. "But there's something going on here in Lorraine and my boys of the Red Ball Express tell me it's the same everywhere just behind the front – all the way from here up into Holland." He held up a white-palmed, coal-black hand. "Don't ask what it is. But the day before yesterday, for example, up near Briey, some limeys appeared out of nowhere and it looks as if they murdered one of our guys. Who were they? Why did they do it?" He shrugged and then dismissed the matter with a curt, "So when the shit hits the fan, Mrs White's handsome son wants to have already taken a powder." He leaned back

* European Theatre of Operations

in the battered chair, complete master of the situation. "All right, if it's a deal," he reached out his hand and Savage shook the dry hard paw automatically, "let's get down to business, eh . . ."

Four

"*A Pole?*" Patton echoed, his voice shaky.

"Yessir," Codman said, noticing for the first time just how old his chief really was. He had seen him on battlefields from North Africa to here in Northern France, but he had never experienced 'Ole Blood an' Guts' as shaken as this. The boss had even accepted a slug of bourbon from his flask and under normal circumstances he never touched a drink of strong alcohol till dinner at the earliest. "Yes, according to the ID they found on what was left of the pilot's body, he was in one of the Polish Air Force squadrons attached to 9th TAC Air. They specialise in low-level ground attacks against enemy armour. Tank busters, they call themselves."

"Well, the Polack bastard nearly frigging well did for my frigging tank!" Patton exclaimed in an attempt at his normal crude, profane humour. "What was wrong with the guy? Couldn't he recognise an L-5 when he saw one? Hell's bells, every goddam artillery outfit in the ETO uses them for spotting Krauts."

Codman gave a little shrug. "I don't know about that, sir. The whole thing's something of mystery. Our people are still investigating." He broke off. Patton wasn't really listening. He was clutching the canteen of bourbon in both white-knuckled hands as if he were afraid he might spill the spirit, staring into nothing.

In a way, Codman, the one-time fighter-pilot himself, could understand the Old Man. That near miss had shaken even him and he'd been used to many a near-miss in the old times. Just when he had tensed, ready for the slugs to start tearing his body to shreds, the pilot had seemed to lose control of the Spitfire, flying at near stalling speed. The British-made fighter had gone down abruptly, as if on some invisible high-speed elevator, struck a tree, bowled over and had gone skidding and screeching upside down across a ploughed field, shredding a crazy wake of ripped metal behind it. A minute later they had landed and he and the pilot had gone running clumsily over the furrows to where the plane lay, thick white smoke pouring out of it, in an attempt to rescue the pilot before the Spitfire burst into flames.

Too late! The Polish pilot was already dead behind the gleaming spider's web of the cockpit's perspex, the steering column skewered through his chest like an animal prepared on a spit for roasting. Hastily the young pilot had reached in and turned off the fuel lines and, for what seemed a long time, they had simply stood there listening to the drip-drip of escaping fuel and the creak of tortured metal trying to reassert itself. Then finally they had commenced trying to find out what was going on.

Now, as Colonel Codman reported to Patton, sitting bolt upright and tense in a chair in the CO's quarters at Etain airfield, he realised that there was pathetically little to relate in reality. For some reason, although they had found the pilot's ID identifying him as a Polish Flying Officer of the Royal Air Force, which had been confirmed by the squadron number on the shattered plane's fuselage, they had been unable to discover his log book or any personal belongings. The dead Polack had not possessed the usual lucky charm that all fighter pilots carried with them – a rabbit's foot or a pair of lady's silk panties and the like. He seemed to have stepped into the plane for his last mission with nothing save his ETO card.

"You'd think," Patton said hesitantly, as the first sad flakes

of new snow came drifting down over that hill where the Battle
of Verdun had brought an end to a European way of life nearly
three decades before, "that he didn't *want* anybody to know
much about him."

"You mean the Pole, sir?"

"Yeah."

Codman considered Patton's words for a few moments
before asking somewhat hesitantly. "What do *you* think, sir?"

Patton didn"t answer immediately. Instead he took another
drink of the bourbon as if he needed the stimulus, before saying
in an unusually subdued manner for him, "I think, Charles, that
that Polack was out to kill yours truly." He had another drink
and avoided looking his aide in the eye.

Codman stared at him aghast. "But who . . . why, sir?" he
stuttered. "How come the Pole—"

"The Krauts," Patton cut him off sharply, shaking his greying
cropped head like a man trying to wake up from a heavy sleep.
"The Krauts were behind it. I think that Pole was working for
them. There are plenty of Polacks in their Armed Forces, as
you well know—"

"But the Spit, sir?" Codman objected.

"Surely they've got a few of those too. Pilots bale out and
leave their planes to find their own way," Patton laughed
shortly, but there was no corresponding warmth in his cold,
calculating eyes. "Pilots have to force land in Kraut territory.
No, neither the pilot nor the plane would be a problem for the
enemy." He paused momentarily, as if the thought had just
come to him and the shock of knowledge made it difficult for
him to express it in words. Finally, however, he managed to
articulate it, saying, "One thing's for sure, Charles, the Krauts
will try again." He drained his drink and stood, stamping his
elegantly booted feet as if to bring life back into them.

"But why, sir . . . why should they attempt to – er – murder
you like this, and at this particular stage of the war? They could

have done it years ago, back in '42 in North Africa if they had wanted to. I can't—"

Patton held up his hand to cut him short. "I don't know is the short answer, Charles." He reached for the lacquered helmet. "Let's forget it, Charles. Let's get on to Eddy's HQ and put a fire up his plump ass." He grinned, displaying those dingy sawn-off teeth of his. We ain't even started earning our pay for this day, you know . . ."

Somewhere up the pot-holed, battle-littered D road an 88mm cannon was banging away at regular intervals like a hammer from hell. Even the veterans on Eddy's staff jumped every time the huge German gun fired. Just as regularly the gun's huge shells slammed into the ruined houses of the US-held part of Metz-les-Maizières. Next to the crossroads, the house in which some damned fool of the US Medical Corps had set up his dressing station shuddered like a destroyer at full speed when its bow hits a wave. Patton was appalled that a corps commander like Eddy would pick an exposed place like this for his Corps HQ. But he knew why he had done so. Eddy wanted to impress on his demoralised doughboys that their commanding general, too, was sharing the dangers of the front. He sighed and decided to keep his helmet on as he entered the little shabby HQ – it would be safer.

Eddy and his staff were crowded into what had once been a kitchen, the window blacked-out with GI blankets, staring at their maps in the white hissing glare of a Coleman lantern.

Hastily they attempted to snap to attention when they saw who was pushing aside the blackout curtain to enter. But Patton waved them to desist saying, in good humour once again, "At ease, gentlemen . . . at ease." He nodded to a red-faced, sweating Eddy. "Fine work, General. Up front like this. Inspiration to the troops. Now then." He put on his nickel-framed glasses, in which he would never be photographed (Generals didn't wear glasses!) and said, "Well, what's the form?"

Eddy nodded to his G-2 and the somewhat flustered colonel launched in to the details of the corps, preparation for the coming attack on Fort Driant. Patton absorbed the information, without even once glancing at the big map spread out in front of him. The details were all in his head; he didn't need to.

"So," he said finally as the colonel ended his briefing, and wishing that damned Kraut cannon would stop firing, "You've decided to come in from the north, to go through the backdoor as it were."

Eddy waited, but said nothing. He knew it wasn't wise to do so at such moments. At planning conferences Patton had a shorter fuse than normal – if that was possible.

"Tricky," Patton mused aloud, staring at the map for the first time. "It's going to be a long approach march, Eddy."

"We're of the opinion, General, that this will put the Krauts off guard. We think they'll believe that we won't attempt a dangerous manoeuvre of that kind."

"Good thinking. But naturally, Eddy, the first thing is to knock out the Führer battery – here." His finger stabbed the map to the north of Fort Driant. "Then your corps can advance without any danger from that particular source. It'll give you the edge over the Kraut."

"I'm hoping so, General," Eddy replied dutifully. He could feel his blood pressure beginning to rise once more. He wasn't just *hoping*, he was damn well *praying* that they'd knock out the Führer battery before the movement of his whole three-division strong corps was discovered. If those great guns weren't, he dare not think that particular scenario for disaster to its logical conclusion.

"What of Savage and his Rangers?" Patton asked suddenly, knowing that that Eddy's whole plan and the fate of his corps depended upon that handful of brave resourceful élite troops.

Eddy's brick-red face changed to the colour of puce. He felt sick. He ought to be resting he told himself, instead of bearing the responsibility for the fate of some 40,000 GIs. "Last report from Major Savage," he clicked his fingers at his G-2 testily.

"States that he has made contact with his means of getting in through the Kraut perimeter at Metz just east of Gravelotte." He bent to the map, as if to show Patton, but the colonel didn't get far; for Patton snapped, "Colonel, I was studying Gravelotte when you were just nasty twinkle in your Pappa's eye. Goddammit I know where Gravelotte is!"

"Sir." The hapless colonel flushed almost the same colour as the sick Eddy. "Since then we've had no further contact with Major Savage and his men."

The news didn't alarm Patton. He knew Savage. He was an independently minded bastard, but he was a fine soldier. He'd do it his own way, damn him, but he'd do it. That was the main point. "All right, thank you Colonel."

The G-2 gave a palpable sigh of relief and Codman felt for him; he knew the feeling well.

"General." It was Eddy. He was looking at Patton in a curious way, almost as if he were seeing the Third Army Commander for the very first time, Codman couldn't help thinking.

"Yes?" Patton said, his mind obviously on what had just been said.

"Could I point out something, General?"

"Why sure. Fire away. What is it?" Patton took in Eddy's fat serious face and thought that the other man might be still worried that he was going to be fired. "And don't get your boiler overheated. I know you're doing your best with all those raw replacements you've taken in to your divs in the last week or so."

"It's not that, General," Eddy said hesitantly.

"Well, what the Sam Hill is it?"

"There are rumours, General," Eddy said uncertainly. "Rumours

45

that the Krauts – well, put it like this, General—" he broke off and took another course. "There's a lot of funny things happening just behind the front these last few days. There were some limeys, for instance—"

"You mean that you think that somebody's aiming to bump me off," Patton interrupted the other general with a huge grin on his craggy face. "Is that it, General, eh?"

Eddy looked at him in total amazement. "How . . . how did you know?" he gasped.

Patton laughed again, though Codman thought the laugh was a little forced. "Rank hath its privileges," he proclaimed. "After all I am the goddam army commander and army commanders get to know such things faster than corps commanders. It's the old army game, you know." He clapped the smaller officer across his bent shoulders. "Don't you worry. The Krauts'll have to get up a mite earlier in the day to crack General George S. Patton. They couldn't in the last show and they won't in this, believe you me."

"Yes, yes . . . of course," Eddy agreed hurriedly, as Patton beamed down at him winningly. "Naturally you're right, sir. You'll go on for ever, sir." But Codman, standing next to the door ready to make a dash with his boss back to the Packard through the damned German cannon fire, was abruptly assailed by the uneasy feeling that General Eddy didn't quite believe his words. Neither did he personally. But there was no time for further reflection. As their own 'Long Toms'* opened fire with a tremendous crash and the counter-battery fire commenced, he yelled "Come, on, sir, let's beat it!"

Patton needed no urging. Boastful and vainglorious as he was, he had a well-developed sense of self-preservation. He was sure he was not going to allow his life to be snuffed out by some random anonymous 88mm shell. He beat it . . .

* 105mm cannon.

*   *   *

Two hundred metres away *Oberleutnant* von Thoma of the *SS Panzerwaffe* watched them flee through his binoculars, praying that a shell might carry the great man off and end his mission without any further ado. But that wasn't to be. Suddenly the *Ami* mortars opened up and smoke shells were exploding everywhere in no-man's land. Swiftly a blinding smoke screen developed into which Patton and his Packard vanished as abruptly as they had appeared. He sighed and put down his glasses.

"Penny for them?" the artillery captain crouching next to him in the shelter of the ruined French barn asked, cupping his hands about his mouth to make himself heard above the thunder of the 88mm cannon.

"Unprintable," von Thoma answered laconically and grinned harshly, though his bright-blue soldier's eyes remained unsmiling. It was a long time since *Oberleutnant* Von Thoma had had anything to smile about. But then the average German 'stubble-hopper' hadn't had much to write home about since Stalingrad back in '42.

"Still, you made the water in the arse of that *Ami* general boil over. Did you see how he hoofed it, *Oberleutnant?*"

"I would have preferred if he hadn't been in a position to – er – hoof it, *Herr Hauptmann.*" Von Thoma answered pulling up the collar of his greatcoat to hide the foreign camouflaged tunic below. He didn't want some fanatical shit of an ex-Hitler Youth arresting him as a spy. In Metz those crazy young cardboard soldiers saw foreign agents everywhere.

"What now?" the artillery captain asked as they doubled back to his battery, where an orderly was dishing out 'nigger sweat' and hunks of 'giddiup sausage'* to ragged, undernourished

---

* Coffee and horsemeat sausage.

gunners crouched in the bottom of the muddy pit, ankle-deep in used shell cases.

"Great crap on the Christmas tree, Captain." Von Thoma caught himself just in time, telling himself he could not let his nerves get the better of him now. "I'm afraid I haven't got a crystal ball or the ability to walk over water." He forced himself to laugh again.

The captain handed him a canteen of the scalding hot, ersatz coffee, "Slip that down past your tonsils and brace yourself for the shock." He winked. "Good shot of schnapps in it."

"Thanks," von Thoma answered and cradled the metal cup gratefully in his frozen hands as he pondered the captain's question. What next? . . . What indeed!

He knew that by the law of averages he should have been dead by the time the *Wehrmacht* had made its bold dash for Kharkov back in the spring of 1942. But somehow he had survived battle after battle ever since he had rolled into Poland back in September 1939, a bright-eyed kid, still wet behind the ears, who had believed he wasn't bringing death but freedom – the freedom of the Führer's New Order – to the downtrodden people of the East.

By now he had been on the bandwagon of war and sudden death far too long. All those young men who had marched with him into Poland in what now seemed another age were long 'looking at the potatoes from below'. He had survived. Von Thoma shivered suddenly.

Opposite him in the trench, with the snow drifting down once more, the artillery officer looked up from his coffee and whipped the dewdrop neatly off the end of his pinched red nose. "Cold?" he queried.

"No," von Thoma answered. "Just somebody standing on my grave . . ."

Five

It had started innocently enough for Kuno von Thoma two months before. He had been recovering in *La Charité*, Berlin, from trenchfoot and a nasty wound in his left thigh, which seemed to take a damned age to heal. As Professor Sauerbruch, Germany's most famous surgeon and chief of the renowned Berlin research hospital, had told him, frowning through his old-fashioned horn-rimmed glasses at the open wound, "Two years ago, my boy, a wound like that should have healed perfectly in a matter of weeks. Now," he had shrugged and puffed out his grey cheeks in a mixture of bewilderment and anger, "who knows? Something to do with stress of war, I suppose."

"More likely the kind of fodder they feed us in the line." He had attempted a joke and winked at *Schwester* Klara, though he had felt as nauseated as always. *Schwester* Klara, who had a fondness for short skirts and sheer silk stockings – quite contrary to regulations – among other things, winked back.

Sauerbruch had bent, pulled back his eyelids and examined his eyeballs. "No jaundice – yet." Then to the utter amazement of his fawning staff crowded around him jostling for places, as if some of the *Herr Professor*'s fame might rub off on them, he pulled out a small bottle of *Korn* and said: "Drink some of this. It might help your liver to do its worst . . . If not, *alter Junge*, you might try this. *Vielleicht kannst Du damit* *eine ruhige Kugel schieben."** With that the Professor and his entourage went, leaving him holding the schnapps and the official-looking note.

He drank the schnapps first, passing the bottle round the little ward of wounded officers. Even 'One Ball', who clutched his stomach every time that someone *else* coughed, had a careful drink of the fiery liquid.

Finally when the officers had settled down for their afternoon nap and *Schwester* Klara had promised, with a wink, 'to plump your pillows for you, little cheetah' later in the evening (and he knew what she meant by 'plumping up his pillow') he unfolded the official message and looked at it.

Outside *La Charité*, all was quiet; even the *Ami* air gangsters had not yet paid their daily visit. The only sounds were the snores of his fellow patients and the cries of the mad officer in the room below, tied to his bed, naked and soiled with his own filth, as usual crying out orders to an infantry company that no longer existed.

The message read:

To all units of the *Wehrmacht*.

The Führer and Commander-in-Chief of the *Wehrmacht* has ordered the formation of special troops for employment in reconnaissance in the West. Approx. strength two war-footing battalions.

Von Thoma had frowned, wondering where this message was leading. Why should the Führer, in charge of millions of soldiers, concern himself with the formation of two small battalions, perhaps just over a thousand men in all? He read on:

All captured US and British equipment and vehicles

* Literally, 'you can push a quiet ball' i.e. cushy number.

are to be surrendered to the Quartermaster-General at once.

Volunteers must be:

(a) physically fit for special duties, intelligent and agile.

(b) fully combat-trained.

(c) have a fluent knowledge of English, including the American dialect, and understand military terms in both English and the American dialect of English . . .

Under other circumstances he would have smiled at that phrase 'American dialect of English.' Momentarily he wondered what his maternal grandfather, the American general and veteran of the US Civil War would have made of that. But not at that particular moment; he had been too puzzled. Hastily he had finished the rest of the strange order, skipping through the words, mind too full of that emphasis on English, a vague suspicion already beginning to unfurl in his brain like a snake freeing itself from its curled state.

. . . This order to be made available to all units *at once.* Volunteers are to report to *Obersturmbannführer* Skorzeny at Friedenthal, Berlin.

Signed KEITEL, Field Marshal.

Von Thoma had known immediately that this new unit requiring volunteers was for him. It smelled of danger, adventure, irregular warfare and, if he had been honest with himself, the final oblivion of death. The name Skorzeny had said it all. Skorzeny, that big, scarfaced Viennese giant had been the man who had snatched the Italian dictator and friend of the Führer, Benito Mussolini, from his mountain-top prison where his fellow Italians had held him captive the previous year; the same man who had recently kidnapped the son of the Hungarian dictator Hortby and used him to blackmail the latter to stay in the war on Germany's side . . . Skorzeny wouldn't be needing linguists for interrogating English-speaking POWs. No there was more to it than that.

Even *Schwester* Klara's blandishments and undoubted sexual charms had not deflected him from his new purpose. If anything she and her wiles had made him more determined to get out of corrupt, war-weary Berlin, while he still had enough willpower and purpose to do so.

That night she had wheeled him out of the ward to see the Professor for a private consultation, watched by his envious fellow officers.

He had passed the English language test with flying colours. Indeed his colloquial English had been more fluent than the *Professor der Anglistik* who had tested him – thanks to his English grandmother and his pre-war school holidays in Bournemouth (which had terminated in 1938 when he had arrived proudly at Victoria, clad in his new Hitler Youth uniform complete with dagger). Indeed the bespectacled Professor, masquerading as a lance-corporal had been impressed by his knowledge of the language and had announced as if he, von Thoma, was one of his graduate students, "I am recommending you for a specialist position."

What that 'specialist position' was to be he didn't find out till afterwards and by then it was too late; he had been committed.

The next stage of his journey had not been to Friedenthal in the north, but in exactly the opposite direction, to the great tank range at Grafenwoehr in remotest Bavaria to the south. But even now the web of deception that would surround the great clandestine operation to come was being woven. His railway pass had read 'Destination – Grafenwoehr'. But the train which had taken him there with other volunteers had never reached the tank-range area. Instead, it had stopped abruptly in what appeared to be the middle of nowhere, near a village station, kilometres away from Grafenwoehr.

There, in the freezing cold, for there was already snow on the mountain peaks, he and the others shivered in the silver blacked-out gloom, wondering why they were here and what the powers-that-be intended for them. As one cocky Berliner, whose shabby field-grey uniform bore no badges of rank, though his skinny chest was covered with tin*, announced, "Comrades, it looks to me as if the clock is in the pisspot again . . . I think I'll go back to the front".

But there was no going back to the front this night or for many a night to come for that matter. In the distance now, echoing around the mountain valley, they could hear the sound of motors labouring through the pass in low gear. Abruptly the tough, hardened faces of the men with von Thoma – veteran survivors to a man, he told himself, from the decorations they bore on their chests – looked animated. They knew the trucks were coming for them. Now, perhaps, they would find out what was going on.

They had been disappointed. Five minutes later the convoy of trucks sent to fetch them pulled up. But there was none of the usual tough banter that took place on such occasions. The drivers didn't respond to their taunts and comments and, to their surprise, a final truck discharged a body of heavily armed SS men who formed a circle around them, their rifles unslung and pointing at the newcomers in an almost menacing manner. "What's this, mate?" the tough cocky Berliner had queried. "You ain't giving us much of a warm welcome, are yer?"

His only reply was from a burly, sour-faced sergeant, who growled, *"Na ponemayu."*

---

* Army slang for medals.

Von Thoma felt a sense of shock. The NCO had answered in *Russian*!

An hour later, after a deliberately confusing ride over back country roads in the Bavarian hinterland, clattering through the silent shuttered hamlets with not even a stray dog in sight (though von Thoma sensed somehow that behind the wooden shutters there were people listening anxiously to their passing – why, he did not know), they arrived at their 'home' for the next weeks.

"Heaven, arse and cloudburst!" one of their number, a naval officer, had exclaimed when he had seen the place. "What's this – a frigging concentration camp or something?"

Von Thoma, who had never seen one of those notorious camps to which, so he had been told, work-shy and political opponents of the Führer were sent to be re-educated, thought it might well be such a place. It was surrounded by triple, high-wire fences, with guard towers at each corner, from which searchlights periodically swept the silent huts the camp contained.

The trucks had halted and their Russian guards, if that was what they were, had commanded hoarsely, "*Davai . . . davai . . .*" slapping the canvas sides of the vehicles to hurry them on; while from the open gate, clearly outlined in the light of the blue lantern hanging there, other SS guards came swarming towards them, restraining fierce open-mouthed Alsatians, saliva dripping from their fangs, with their chains.

"Nice bunch o' poodles," someone commented. But the guards either didn't understand or didn't want to. Using their menacing half-wild brutes of dogs, they forced the bewildered volunteers through the gates, which clanged with an air of finality as the blue lantern went out abruptly "God protect all who enter here," the cocky Berliner intoned solemnly.

They weren't amused.

Six

The next few weeks in this remote sealed-off Bavarian camp passed in hectic activity. The *Kommandokompanie*, to which von Thoma and the other volunteers of that strange night were assigned, was kept going from morning to night. Their only free time was two hours on Sunday afternoon when a mobile brothel arrived probably from the great range at Grafenwoehr and they were allowed the pleasure of one of the whores; and even then they weren't completely off duty. For the whores spoke English of a kind (some said Rommel had brought them back with him from one of the brothels in North Africa where they had catered for the buck-teethed Tommies) and they were expected to speak English to them. As the cocky Berliner exclaimed, "Holy strawsack, you're even expected to do yer frigging homework when yer slipping 'em a nice length of good German salami. What a frigging life!" No one had laughed at the sally. Life was becoming too difficult in this strange place – and they were beginning to grow worried.

Every morning started, after the usual tough physical training, with the showing of captured US Signals Corps films and Hollywood movies. But after the first two weeks, a group of them were segegrated from the rest and were shown British war films – *Next of Kin*, *Desert Victory* and the like which weren't as exciting as the American ones. "The *Amis* have blondes in the bombers," the Berliner, who naturally had to be called 'Schulze'*, complained. "Not even a shifting glimpse of a bit o' female titty."

Not that they were particularly interested in 'a bit o'female titty'. They were too tired from the constant round of physical activity, the learning of new techniques and the bruising routine of unarmed combat. Put them in a darkened room with a relatively comfortable seat and they were fast asleep within minutes.

As November began to approach, they were paraded to the quartermaster's stores, where Meier, the chief 'quartermaster bull' confronted them with heaps of olive drab uniform pieces, all obviously captured from the *Amis* or taken from their dead – they could see the stained patched places, where the late owner had been hit, quite clearly.

"Lovely material," the gross quartermaster bull with the Jewish features had proclaimed, fingering the nearest pair of US woollen pants fondly. "Don't make that kind of stuff in the Reich these days, you can take that from me. No ersatz here. All pure wool."

"Bavarian barnshitter," Schulze had whispered, "the old Yid is gonna cream hissen in half a mo."

"You can even try the black market, but stuff like this—" the fat quartermaster had caught sight of von Thoma and had stopped abruptly, as he seemingly recognised the harshly handsome young soldier with the livid, fresh scar slashed down his right cheek. "*Oberleutnant* von Thoma," he had said, using von Thoma's name and military rank, the first time it had been used in this strange camp (instead they had been renamed 'Harry', 'Elmer', 'Hiram' and the like) "Over here for you and your comrades," he had meant the men who had shared the same hut as von Thoma.

Puzzled even more, the group had allowed themselves to be led into a separate room, where again there was a pile of captured equipment, but this was the military booty from a different army.

* A typical Berlin name

"Tommy," Schulze had spotted the difference immediately in that customary, sharp-eyed Berlin manner of his.

"*Genau*," Meier had agreed. "Not as good as that from the *Amis*, but still good quality—"

"Oh get on with it," von Thoma had snapped, losing patience. He had hated the bull's drooling about the superiority of the enemy equipment; it reminded him yet again that Germany had virtually lost the war.

Mcicr had flushed and then he said sourly, "All right, *Herr Oberleutnant*, would you and your men try on those uniforms over there for size – *please*."

Von Thoma had been too surprised at the 'you and your men' – did it mean, *he* was in command of the couple of dozen men from varied units all around him? – to comment on Meier's tone. Instead he strode over to the uniforms, still smelling of the ammonia which had been used to clean them, and stared at them.

They were camouflaged, somewhat in the manner of the camouflage used by the *Waffen SS*'s own infantry, but it was the beret that was attached to each uniform and the badge on it which was completely new to him. It was in the shape of a blue-and-white dagger flanked by two upraised wings. Did that mean these uniforms and berets had been taken off dead parachutists? He knew that British airborne troops wore red berets, though these were more of a maroon colour. "What do you make of them, Schulze?" he asked his neighbour.

Schulze, comedian as always, snapped to attention as if he were still a recruit, hands tucked in tightly to the side of his trousers and bellowed "Beg to report, *Herr Oberleutnant* that Sergeant Schulze is not wont to walk across the water and have visions. He doesn't frigging well know, *Herr Oberleutnant*."

Von Thoma had grinned and Schulze had grinned back, saying in his normal tone, "Got to get used to the old bullshit once more, sir. Now that you're our superior officer."

The former had made an obscene gesture and Schulze had snapped, "'Fraid, no can do, sir. Already got a double-decker bus up there, *sir.*" Then he relaxed and said, "Some kind of Tommy special outfit I suppose, sir. The Tommies go in for that kind of stuff. They're allus going off on raids and the like in special units out on a lark."

"Lark is the wrong word for it, Sergeant Schulze," a Viennese-accented voice cut in in that decidedly unmilitary manner of the Austrians.

They swung round and clicked to attention as one. There was no mistaking that massive figure standing in the doorway, towering above all of them by a head, his scarred face tilted to one side quizzically, as if he were mustering them – and their surprised looks – and was amused by what he saw.

Oberleutnant von Thoma had recovered almost immediately. He had bowed stiffly, raised his right hand to his peaked cap in salute and barked in parade-ground fashion. *"Oberleutnant von Thoma und zwanzig Mann meldet sich zur Stelle, Obersturmbannführer!"*

Skorzeny, the scar-faced giant who had rescued Mussolini and whose photograph had appeared on the front page of every paper in Germany – and not only in Germany – thereafter, returned his salute casually and had said, "At Ease, *Oberleutnant* . . . at ease." He indicated the uniforms. "British," he explained. "British uniforms from their second SAS battalion."

"SAS battalion, sir?"

"Special Air Service, *Leutnant* . . . the model for my own *Jagdkommando** if the truth were known."

The information was received by the assembled volunteers in absolute silence. None of them there, mostly from the eastern front, had ever heard of the Tommy unit. Yet the fact

* Hunting Commando, the SS's own equivalent of the British formation.

58

that Skorzeny himself had revealed the details of it to them personally seemed to them significant; and at that moment more than one of them felt a cold finger of fear trace its way down their spine. What in three devils' name had they volunteered for?

It was almost as if the Austrian giant, with the sabre-scarred face that looked like the work of a butcher's apprentice who had gone mad, could read their minds. For he said, "What has this got to do with me, you might well ask." He smiled at them, but there was no accompanying warmth in his dark eyes which hinted at Slav blood in the Skorzeny lineage. "What am I supposed to do in the uniform of an enemy Tommy outfit? Eh?"

He paused and then, not answering his own question, posed another one. "If you want to kill an opponent in fencing without too much fuss where do you aim your sabre?" He doubled up his mighty right fist as if it might well be clutching the fencing sabre of his student duelling days in Vienna. "You haven't the strength for a long *mensur**. You have to dispatch your opponent in the quickest and most efficient manner possible – one that saves time and effort. So where do you aim your blade?"

Von Thoma hesitated. He didn't like this kind of questioning. The man was toying with them. He had that supercilious attitude of quite ordinary people, who have suddenly gained power or influence and feel that gives them the right to toy with people, as if they are very superior and exceedingly intelligent individuals. "Frankly," he snapped, deciding that it was necessary to show his independence and that of his men right from the start, "we don't know, *Obersturmbann-führer*."

"Of course, of course," Skorzeny said hastily, smiling,

---

* Name given to a student duel at German universities.

though it was obvious that the Austrian giant hadn't liked von Thoma's response. "How could you? You have never fenced, I see." He gestured towards the younger man's pale face.

Von Thoma said nothing. He could have said that by the time he had been eighteen, he had already been wounded in action twice and had had no time for fooling around on the student *paukboden*, the fencing ring, cheered on by a bunch of beer-swilling students.

"Well, I shall tell you," Skorzeny said, seeing that he was not going to get a rise out of the other officer with his tough, no-nonsense soldier's face. "You go for the head. The heart, the stomach, the lungs and the rest of the important organs are too well protected. Even if you do cut them, the opposition takes time to die – perhaps even recovers. But a hearty swipe across the opponent's head, right down through the scalp into the brain puts paid to him for good." He licked his thick sensual lips, as if savouring that killing blow with a razor-sharp sabre blade.

Skorzeny's words were met by absolute silence. Even the dullest, most slow-witted of the volunteers knew they were dealing with a killer. Beneath that superficial Viennese charm, there was a ruthless murderer who would stop at nothing. Their lives didn't count a fig with such a man. There and then, von Thoma swore he wouldn't allow his men to be sacrificed needlessly so that this giant facing them, waiting expectantly for a reaction, could achieve yet more glory from the blood-stained hands of his fellow Austrian, Adolf Hitler.

Skorzeny flashed a look at the open door. No one was listening. All the same he was careful. After all he had sworn a personal oath to the Führer the previous month that he would reveal nothing of the great new offensive on pain of death. And he knew that Hitler would not hesitate to have that penalty carried out if he, Skorzeny, failed to keep his word. With a swift kick of the heel of his boot, he slammed the door closed.

Lowering his voice, as if, even now, he was afraid that someone might overhear him, he said, *"Meine Herren,* what I am to say to you now must not go further than this room. *Verstanden?"*

They nodded they had understood and von Thoma wondered what was coming now, though instinctively he knew, too, that the reason for their being in this remote, strange camp in the back of beyond was now finally about to be revealed to them.

"Germany is soon to go over to the offensive in the West—"

There were stifled cries of surprise and shock at his announcement and Skorzeny held up his hands for immediate silence. "The Führer, in his infinite wisdom, has decided that the time is ripe to throw the Western Allies back into the sea whence they came. Naturally," he mustered them with those dark wicked Slav eyes of his, "it won't be easy. The enemy outnumbers us. He has overwhelming superiority in the air and on the ground in artillery and armour." He let his words sink in before adding, "But remember what I said about striking the enemy's head at fencing. Extinguish the brain," he uttered the words slowly through almost gritted teeth as if it were giving him pleasure to say them, "and the rest falls dead and useless of its own volition. That is what we – *you –* are going to do in the name of Folk, Fatherland and Führer." He drew himself up and thrust out his massive chest, as if he were leading some great final victory parade, marching past the Führer himself.

Inwardly angry, von Thoma attempted to deflate the pompous, self-important bastard, "And what particular head are we supposed to sabre off, *Obersturmbannfüher?"* he asked and next to him, Schulze smiled maliciously. He knew that Skorzeny was getting up his new chief's aristocratic hooter.

"Perhaps you have heard of the 'Cowboy General', *Oberleutnant?"*

Von Thoma shook his head. "Well this *Ami,* who boasts

twin pistols like a Western hero and tends to slap his soldiers if they become reluctant heroes," Skorzeny smiled softly at the thought, "is now commander of the US Third Army which the Führer and his planners think will play a decisive role in the coming battle – *if* we let it."

Outwardly von Thoma remained apparently unmoved. In reality, his brain raced madly, as he guessed what Skorzeny was hinting at.

"But we are *not* going to let it move and play that decisive role, are we? For before this *Ami* Third Army receives its call for action to come and help its hard-pressed comrades in the north, the head of that particular Cowboy General must roll." He smiled, obviously pleased with himself.

"His name?" von Thoma demanded curtly.

"George Patton!"

PART II

A soldier who won't fuck, won't fight.
General Patton

One

"General, they're coming up to the start line now, sir," Codman announced over the stready drumfire of the guns.

Patton, standing on the bonnet of the jeep in the middle of the wet dripping field, raised his big binoculars. Automatically he noted the red flares sailing into the grey sombre sky above the German positions. The Krauts – as always – were waiting. He cursed but didn't take his attention from his front.

Now the line of hesitant Shermans started to churn their way across the muddy fields. Their 75mm cannon twitched from side to side like the snouts of predatory monsters. Behind them came the infantry. Little clusters, the men with their bodies bent as if they were facing a stiff headwind. Here and there officers spoke quietly into their walkie-talkies. Others waved their grease guns, as if in encouragement. Patton told himself that it was like watching a newsreel, one of those grainy jerky silent ones of the Old War when, he, too, had been wounded in these same damp Lorraine fields. "Shot in the ass, gentlemen," he had often announced at drunken Friday evenings in some goddam peacetime officers' club. "Here let me show you." And he would peel down his pants to show his fellow officers the great gnarled hole in his right buttock. "Inch or two more and I'd have been singing counter tenor." It had always been good for a laugh in those awful, boring peacetime days.

But all that was forgotten now as he watched the real thing

65

once more. On the top of the other jeep, red-faced General Eddy swung his glasses round to view the closest of the forts protecting Fort Driant. Reluctantly, Patton did the same. He knew they had to go through with this real-life exercise for what was to come later. But he didn't like it – not one bit. After all, some poor mother's son was gonna get killed testing their plans.

For a moment or two, till the fog of war drifted in again, he caught a glimpse of one of the 1870 forts, its squat outline silent as yet, but sinister. The very stone seemed to exude menace. Then the low single-storey structure disappeared into the smoke of the artillery barrage like a ship slipping away on a winter ocean.

The thunder of the guns had reached a crescendo now. Officers shouted unheard by the watching generals. The infantry crouched even lower. All of them seemed to be chewing. "Like goddam sheep tamely going to the slaughter," Patton told himself grimly. The tanks churned on. For how much longer was anybody's guess.

Next to him Codman bit his bottom lip. The tension was awful. To any casual observer the fort seemed abandoned, harmless, a military ruin left over from another century, the circles of torn barbed wire on its roof long eaten away by red rust. He knew differently. Up there, there were men equally tense and determined as the attackers. They, too, waited for the bloody drama to commence, once the bombardment would cease. The only difference was that they were protected by minefields and concrete walls some two yards thick.

Suddenly – startlingly – a green flare soared through the grey sky over the top of the Shermans, which were already slowing down noticeably. It was the signal. Patton stiffened. Opposite, on the other jeep, Eddy did the same. They waited for the fire storm. Below, the infantry had almost reached the

base of the fort. The Shermans, apparently unable to scale the
fort's steep glacis wall, were breaking to left and right. They'd
make smoke, Patton knew, in a moment and hope to get away
before the bloody slaughter began.

Next moment the whole of the US XII Corps artillery –
six hundred guns of all calibres – thundered into action in
one great devastating, frightening, earth-shaking roar. Automatically Patton and Codman opened their mouths to prevent
their eardrums from bursting. The blast whipped their uniforms about their bodies. A hot wind buffeted their faces
like a blow from a soft, damp fist. They blinked and blinked
again.

With a hoarse, exultant scream the second salvo of shells
shot over their heads like some racketing express train roaring
at full speed through an empty midnight station. Salvo after
salvo followed. The first terrifying sighs turned swiftly into
one long baleful howl. It rose and rose and rose in an elemental
fury that seemed to go on for ever.

The skirmish line of trenches below the fort's summit
vanished in an instant. Barbed wire was chopped and hacked
like cooked spaghetti. Great chunks of red-hot shrapnel scythed
lethally through the yellow-grey fog of artillery smoke. To
the right of the fort, already disappearing in the smoke,
there was a sudden cherry-red flash. Perhaps a POL* dump
going up. Elsewhere rippling fires broke out. Patton could
have sworn that the great fort shook and trembled like a
live thing.

Patton turned his glasses back to the men still toiling
forward. His hands trembled as he did so. Soon there would
be the moment of truth. He knew it. The advancing infantry
knew it, even the thickest of them. In a moment their fate,
perhaps the rest of their lives, would be decided: whether they

* Fuel dump.

were maimed or not; stamped as a 'yellow-bellied coward'; died or lived . . .

As abruptly as it had started the Corps barrage and with it the rest of the covering fire ceased. Behind it, remained a loud echoing silence which reverberated around the circle of surrounding hills.

Suddenly the infantry were on their own. For a moment or two, they ceased the fearful plodding forward to their inevitable fate. Not for long, however. Whistles shrilled. Red-faced noncoms shouted angrily. Company commanders yelled that dreaded, familiar rallying cry, "Okay, guys . . . let's go! . . . GET THE LEAD OUTA YA ASSES . . . LET'S GO!"

As if a spell had been broken, the infantry streamed forward in ragged lines. They screamed; they shrieked; they yelled. It was as if they were being carried away by some primeval, unreasoning lust – the lust to make someone pay for their suffering; the lust to kill.

"God, what a spectacle," Patton breathed in awe, all posturing and posing vanished before that sight. "There's nothing like it . . . *nothing!*"

Somewhere in the drifting yellow smoke, the first German machine gun burst into action. A long high-pitched hysterical burst. Tracer cut the fog. The first line was ripped apart. GIs went down on all sides. Men clutched the air with clawed hands, screaming at their fate, determined not to go down. Others fell silent and lay there in the ploughed earth as if they had abruptly gone to sleep. A GI wearing nickel issue-glasses sat down with a start. His glasses slipped absurdly to one ear. For all the world he looked like a joke, a man who had skidded on a banana to the amusement of spectators.

But no one was amused this terrible killing morning. Everywhere the cries went up, pitiful in their bloody misery, "Medic . . . medic . . . For Chrissake, help me, medic," as a blinded soldier walked straight into that lethal fire which had erupted everywhere now.

Codman groaned. He put down his binoculars. He could look no more. Patton acted. Not lowering his glasses for an instant, he shouted above the battle to the officer crouched over his radio in the back of the jeep. "Get those Shermans back in action, for Chrissake! . . . I'll shoot their fucking CO personally, if he has not got the goddam cowardly pricks moving in sixty seconds!"

"Yessir!" the officer snapped and bent immediately over his radio.

While Patton fumed and Codman fought off the temptation to clap his hands over his ears and drown out the terrible sounds of misery and mayhem coming from the men being slaughtered over at the fort, the first Shermans started to crawl out of the dead ground. They were buttoned up, Codman could see that and he could visualise the apprehension of the five-man crews in their jolting, rattling steel boxes as they joined the battle.

The lead Shermans fired first. A streak of angry red. Next instant a blur of speeding white. An armour-piercing shell, solid steel all the way through. Codman groaned. It bounced off one of the fort's cupolas like a glowing golf ball. It had not even made an impression on the steel.

Next second the fort's major defences cracked into action. It was as if the place's devilish, unseen gunners had been using the stalled US infantry to lure the tanks into attacking. Everywhere scarlet flame stabbed the grey gloom. 'Moaning minnies' howled, the shells from the six-barrelled, electric mortars streaking straight into the sky before plunging down at a tremendous rate onto the waddling tanks, attempting to crawl up the slope in low gear.

The tankers didn't stand a chance. The first Sherman came to an abrupt. halt. A crewman flung open the turret. Through their glasses, the awe-struck observers could see the panic-struck man slump over the rim of the turret, blue greedy flames already consuming the rest of his charred body. No one else attempted to get out. Slowly a great ring of black, oily smoke started to ascend into the sky.

Another Sherman shuddered to a stop, track flopping out behind it. A third was hit at close range. The ten-ton turret sailed lazily through the smoke like a kids' toy. That did it. The remaining Shermans of the first wave turned tail and scuttled back the way they had come.

Still the brave infantry kept on trying. Through the great gaps carved out of their ranks, the engineers charged forward. They carried with them long bamboo poles like boys do when they bait rabbits in their burrows. Behind them came the volunteers, each man covered by a bodyguard armed with a tommy gun. In their hands they carried a short length of hose. On their back a large round pack bumped up and down as they pounded up the shell-cratered slope. They were flame-thrower operators. They knew that every defender would be bringing his fire to bear upon them as soon as they were spotted. Not one of the defenders would have the slightest hesitation in mowing them down. Everyone hated the soldiers with the flame throwers.

The engineers, panting and gasping, flung themselves down. Here and there they were hit even as they did so. Still the survivors persisted. They poked their long poles under the tangles of shattered barbed wire, thrusting the explosive charges as close as they could to the bunkers. Bullets thwacked viciously into the churned up earth all around them.

"Go and get 'em, boys," Patton cried enthusiastically as the first charges started to explode, showering the crawling infantry with great clods of earth and pebbles.

Now it was the turn of the men with the flame throwers. They sprang through the gaps in the wire, hoses already hissing furiously like some deadly snake ready to strike. The first sheet of flame sprang forward. It slapped the nearest bunker with a hard thwack. For a moment it embraced the bunker, turning it an evil dull-glowing red. Steam and smoke rose. The flame receded. Behind it it left a line of charred black on the ground. The bunker machine gun fell silent.

"We're gonna do it," Patton yelled exuberantly, as another of the volunteers went to work with his fearsome weapon. "We've got the Krauts on the—"

The words died on his lips. The flame thrower operator had been caught by burst of machine-gun fire in mid-stride. Savagely it tore him in half. The frightening impact swung the dying man round, but in his hands, the gun fired. Bright-red sizzling flame crackled along the line of infantry following him up the hill. They fell on all sides. Desperately they tried to beat out the greedy rising flames with hands that were already on fire and turning instantly into shrivelled blackened claws. To no avail. They writhed and died, their struggles getting weaker by the instant as those greedy, all-consuming flames turned them into charred pygmies.

Now the enemy turned the full weight of their firepower on the hapless Americans, many of them wandering around on the pitted glacis of the fort in confusion, weaponless, like lunatics sudenly released from the asylum and not knowing what to do with their new freedom. On the grey smudged horizon, yellow lights, ugly and threatening, flickered abruptly. Patton and the other spectators of the slaughter caught their breath expectantly, knowing instinctively that something terrible was going to happen. There was a sound like the *Chicago Chief* tearing down the track at a hundred miles per hour. In a flash the whole wide world seemed filled with that terrible, awe-inspiring sound. Next instant the first salvo landed right on the roof of the enemy-held fort. Even at that distance, the spectators could feel the earth tremble under that awesome impact.

Ancient trees sailed into the air. A Sherman flew into space, a kid's tin toy. Another, crawling towards the low concrete

71

mass, was swept away like an irksome fly being swatted by some invisible hand. Now the survivors started to stream back as that terrible long-range cannon thundered from Fort Driant. Flinging away their weapons, hobbling with the aid of their comrades, thrusting and jostling one another in their unreasoning panic, they fled back past the observers.

"Oh, my God," Codman gasped, face suddenly ashen. "It's a massacre!"

It was. Even Patton, who rarely tolerated failure, realised that. He bellowed at the sweating, harassed radio operator. Frantically he started to send his recall signals. Here and there officers and senior noncoms tried to stop the rot. Like angry children in a playground, they spread their linked arms and attempted to halt the flight to the rear. To no avail! The survivors simply couldn't be stopped. Eyes wild, white and staring, saliva dribbling from slack mouths, mumbling meaningless phrases or sobbing, they pushed by the stop line. Patton, face grey, but thin cheeks flushed a hectic pink, turned away, as if he couldn't bear to see them any more. "Smoke," he cried above the boom-boom of the enemy guns, "bring down some goddam smoke!"

Moments later the first smoke shells started to explode around the defiant enemy fort. The attack had failed. The experiment, using all arms, had not worked. Now it was up to Savage and his Rangers. If they couldn't go in by the front door, they'd have to use the back, damn it!

"Take the bastard away," Patton barked at his driver. "Let me get away from this goddam place."

The driver acted immediately. He thrust home first gear. Without waiting to ascertain Eddy's reaction, Patton shot away, slumped huddled in his seat, his face empty of emotion. Suddenly, George S. Patton, the famed commander of the Third Army, looked very old . . .

Two

"In five klicks we hit Thionville," Whitey said, pointing to the shattered *Wehrmachat* sign, next to the shot-up Panther, already rusting, with the legend stencilled on it *Diedenhofen.* "Kraut for Thionville. All the places around here have Kraut and Frog names."

"I know," Savage said baldly, as the jeep sped smoothly along at the head of the Red Ball Express convoy, watched by the tall bored MPs.

"You know a lot of things, Major," Whitey said with a grin, showing those beautiful white teeth of his like an ad. for Colgate toothpaste. "Still I'm a colonel and you're only a major. So you can't be *that* smart."

Now, preoccupied as he was, it was Savage's turn to grin. The big black was a card. For now he was dressed as a very elegant bird colonel, totally unlike the louche pfc. he had been when Savage had first met him in the dive in Montmédy's red-light district. The only thing that marred his appearance were the sunglasses he affected despite the wintry weather. But he had a purpose in wearing the glasses, too. "Keep those Army cops off'n my back. A nigger who wears dark glasses on duty must be a tough hombre, they figure. Just an angle, you know, Major."

And by now Savage was beginning to think that Whitey, who had left school in eighth grade, knew all the angles – and then some. He turned and looked back. The White scout car with

73

his Rangers was keeping its distance, just behind the second supply truck. He could even make out Hairless Harry's bald head as he carried out his thrice daily routine of rubbing Bay Rum and Bourbon into his naked skull. To no purpose. His hair never grew. His grin broadened and he turned back to Whitey. "What happens then, er, *Colonel*, sir?"

"At Thionville?"

"Yeah."

"This jeep has a breakdown . . . fan belt, something simple like that. It leaves the convoy. Your guys follow. Coin of the realm changes hands and Whitey, suitably rewarded for his patriotic efforts on behalf of good ole Uncle Sam, departs happily to leave you, Major to go on your merry way."

"You're a cynic, Whitey, do you know?"

"So they tell me, Major. But I don't lose much sleep over the fact. Us niggers, as you well know," suddenly his accent had become a thick southern goo, one hundred per cent 'Rastus', "is a happy-go-lucky bunch o'coons. Not a care in the frigging world." There was the bitterness, Savage told himself. Very definitely so. He wondered momentarily what kind of life it must be for an intelligent black in the south, where even now it was wise for a 'nigra' to keep his coon mouth closed, speak only when spoken to, if he didn't want some redneck lynching party to close his mouth for good.

To the south in the direction of Metz the guns continued to thunder and he told himself Patton's Third was out of luck. Those were Kraut heavies and there was no retaliatory fire from the US artillery. The knowledge gave his next question some urgency. "How far are these – er – friends of yours prepared to take us, Whitey?"

"As far as your dough goes – well almost that far. They aim to survive the war. They're gonna leave the heroic dying for noble causes to your soldier boys, Major."

"And very wise of them, too," Savage humoured the bitter, cynical, black man.

Half an hour later, the big fat black who acted as the 'colonel's shoffer' fooled the MP sergeant in charge of the Red Ball Express crossroads, where the roads led north to Luxembourg City and south to German-held Metz. "Niggers," he said to himself, eyes raised to the heavens as if in prayer, "back home with not a pot to piss in and hardly able to handle a mule and here they give 'em a jeep. What can you expect? They'd fuck up a Model T Ford, they're so goddam dumb. Kay off the highway".

"Yes Cap'n . . . you're right there, Cap'n," the driver agreed, again doing that Rastus act that all Whitey's men seemed able to perform at the drop of a hat – "Play the dumb nigger and white trash is happy," Whitey had explained, "makes 'em feel more smart."

Now the lone jeep followed by the White scout car was limping away from the houses on the outskirts of Thionville heading for the slag heaps and pit shafts that blackened the countryside to the north of Metz and the battlefield beyond. And suddenly both the jeep driver and his boss had dropped their slow-moving black good-for-nothing carelessness. They were all eyes, and Savage knew why. This was Indian country. One wrong move and you were dead!

It was growing dark when the jeep stopped. Behind them in the scout car, Hairless Harry dropped almost noiselessly to the gravel on the path which surrounded the apparently abandoned house, its slate roof holed everywhere, probably during some artillery bombardment. Immediately without an order from the bald man, the Rangers formed a defensive semi-circle. Veterans that they were, they acted instinctively. After all, time and time again they had survived because they had been a few seconds quicker than their enemies.

Whitey, who had already loosened the big .45 in his leather

holster, said in a low voice, all banter vanished now. "This is it. This is where we make contact, Major. Have the greenbacks ready. These guys think in dollar signs."

In single file, the three of them, the black-market boss in the lead, entered the house – probably it had once belonged to some prosperous mill owner who had fled with the Germans before the advancing Americans back in the previous September.

They crunched across the broken glass and slates in the entrance hall. The furniture once plump and plush had been ripped open by looting GIs with their trench knives and bayonets. Probably they had thought it contained a fortune. They moved past a picture of Hitler, riddled with bullet holes, a swastika carved crudely across the stern face. Above, raindrops dripped mournfully from a shell hole in the ceiling. All was waste, destruction and foreboding, as if somewhere in the old rambling place there was someone or something waiting to surprise them.

Savage didn't like the look, or feel, of the place one bit, but Whitey and the black corporal driver seemed perfectly at ease there. He soon realised why. There were bits and pieces of what the GIs called 'goodies' everywhere among the damp mess of the supposed abandoned house: half-eaten Hershey bars, ripped-open packs of *Camels* and *Lucky Strikes*, a couple of brown GI blankets and even a can of gasoline. He kicked it to test its contents – it was full and probably worth a small fortune on the French black market, where most vehicles were *gazogenes*.* He turned to Whitey. "You've been here before – several times," he said. It wasn't a question, but a statement.

"Sure," Whitey answered easily, as somewhere in the direction of Metz another salvo from the heavies made the place

---

* Gas-driven vehicles, powered by a huge bag of the stuff carried on the roof or in a trailer towed behind.

shake so much that a slate fell through the gaping hole in the roof.

"So this is where you meet your contacts – the guys who are going to help us—"

"For a fee," Whitey interjected mildly.

"Yeah for a fee. But why meet them here – your contacts I mean? It's very close to the front and dangerous."

Whitey shrugged. "Crossing the street is dangerous, Major," he said carelessly, as if it were not important, but Savage noted that the corporal standing behind him looked worried. He raised his voice. "Because it's dangerous, the MPs don't sashay down here, poking their long noses into things. So we just have a breakdown with one of the trucks. It goes to the workshop for a quick fix. But in reality it comes down here and gets rid of its load in double-quick time."

"Yes, yes, I can understand that. But why do the Frogs risk their necks in this goddam place? If the Krauts sent out a patrol from Metz and collared them, they'd be in real trouble, found with US goodies."

For the first time since he had met him in Montmédy, Whitey looked uneasy and Savage thought he knew why. Hastily, he hit home. "But then it's the Krauts that your Frogs are selling our stuff to, isn't it?"

Behind Savage, Hairless Harry, his self-appointed body-guard gasped. And Hairless Harry, a bootlegger during Pro-hibition was not exactly a Caspar Milquetoast.

Whitey looked serious. "I guess so. As long as they pay in greenbacks, Major, I've never bothered myself too much with that kind of thing." His voice took on a more aggress-ive tone. "After all, Major Savage, we black guys are not supposed to be too bright in the top storey, are we? We can't follow things like that if you don't draw us a pic-ture—"

"Cut the crap," Savage interrupted him brutally. "So what's

the deal? I'm not risking the lives of my guys until I know what kind of ante we're playing for. Do you understand?"

But before the handsome black deserter and black marketeer could answer, there was that well-known sound of a rifle bolt being drawn back. The four of them spun round as one.

Savage crouched low, hand flashing to his .45 instinctively. But he never got there. The civilian standing in the shattered doorway, jerked up his German machine pistol and said, voice toneless, but menacing all the same, "*Ça suffit, hein!*"

"Shit on shingle," Hairless Harry cried. "Bushwhacked!" He lowered his carbine.

Now Whitey took over for he obviously knew the stranger who had sprung the surprise on them in this remote place, with the guns thundering ominously outside and the steady mournful drip-drip coming from the shattered roof. "*Bonjour, Pepé,*" he said with fake enthusiasm, "*ça va?*"

"*Ça va,*" the stranger with the unshaven face and shifty, wary dark eyes answered, his mouth worked as if by rusty steel springs. "You got?" he added in accented English.

"I got," Whitey answered promptly. "The trucks already stopped two kilometres back up the road. Full of goodies." He beamed at the Frenchman, but his eyes didn't light up. Savage could see the Negro wasn't too happy with his contact man either. Whitey's voice rose and he thrust out his right hand to indicate Savage and Hairless Harry. "These are the gentlemen, I told you about. They are to go with you."

The Frenchman, still holding his rifle levelled at the four Americans standing in the wet rubble of the shattered house, gave Savage a sour look. "You got money?" he asked.

Savage nodded.

"*Bon*, I take." Now he lowered his rifle and Savage could see why. There were other shadowy armed figures outside, too. He wasn't alone. "Make ready."

"Hold it," Savage said, as the man appeared about to turn and move out. "How far are you taking us and how safe is it?"

"*Environs*, near," the Frenchman named Pepe corrected himself, "Mazières-les-Metz. The Boche are in strength, there."

Savage nodded his understanding. "How do we get there?"

"We walk. It is better. We know the way – way the Boche do not know." He said the words with an air of finality and without waiting for any further questions stalked back to the others outside, obviously ready to give them their instructions concerning Whitey's black-market truck from the Red Ball Express. Idly Savage wondered what it contained. Then he dismissed that particular problem. From what little he had seen of Pepe and his rogues he had got more than enough problems on his hands already. He flashed a look at Hairless Harry. The latter nodded his head in agreement. The look on his broad tough face said everything – those guys'd sell their own mother for a couple of dimes. He went out to raise the others.

Savage was left alone with Whitey, who looked strangely uneasy (for that particular, cool customer). He said nothing. But Whitey answered his unspoken question. "Watch your back, Major," he said drily and then in an even stranger manner for that angry black marketeer, he reached out his hand and said, "Shake, if you would sir—"

Five minutes later they were on their way to the unknown.

Three

The man had had Gestapo written all over him, von Thoma had told himself as they had paraded in front of Skorzeny in their strange new camouflaged uniforms. Tall, well fed, middle aged, cunning, all-knowing eyes; a stump of a cheap working-man's cigar clenched between his gold teeth at the corner of his crooked mouth. When he had walked on the little parade ground next to Skorzeny, his ankle-length, green-leather coat had creaked audibly. Now at a nod from Skorzeny he had commenced walking down the three ranks of what was now known as 'the L-Squad'. What the 'L' stood for, von Thoma didn't know. Soon he'd find out.

The Gestapo man took his time, staring at each man, as if he were some keen-eyed 'drill bull' during recruit training, looking for the slightest fault so that he could 'make a sow' out of the unfortunate recruit. A couple of times he stared at their berets and shook his head as if in disapproval, whispering out of the side of his slack sensual mouth, "Colour washed out. Red . . . should be more maroon."

"Will be changed forthwith," Skorzeny had said and made a note of the point on his pad as if he were some long-time 'rear echelon stallion' instead of the commander of the biggest bunch of rogues that von Thoma had ever come across in the whole of his career in the *Wehrmacht*.

Finally the two of them had been satisfied and Skorzeny had stood them at ease, while he introduced the Gestapo

80

cop. *"Oberkommissar Hartwig, Geheime Staatspolizei.* He'll say a few words to you now." He nodded at the cop. Slowly, deliberately the cop took the wet stub of cigar out of his mouth and said, as if he had all the time in the world, fixing them with those suspicious cop eyes of his, "The boys back at HQ call me the 'Mummy's Voice'. Why?" He answered his own strange question. "Cos I can bring even a mummy to sing like a little yeller canary." He chuckled, but there was no warmth in the sound. "So when they brought the Tommies up in front of me down there in Alsace, they gave me the usual crap – rank, name and number – and no more. Huh!" He spat contemptuously on the frozen concrete of the parade ground. "Half an hour later, they're pissing themsens, babbling away like frigging old slack cunts."

Von Thoma frowned. So did Skorzeny. Good Nazi that he was, he obviously didn't like that kind of talk all the same. But then, von Thoma told himself, the cop had probably served the Kaiser loyally, then the Weimar Republic, now Hitler. If the Reds ever took over in Germany, he'd serve them too to the best of his ability – as long as they paid his pension in due course.

"Get on with it, please *Herr Oberkommissar,*" Skorzeny snapped.

"*Jawohl, Obersturmbannführer,*" the cop answered, in no way put out. Nothing and nobody impressed him; his old rheumy, cunning eyes had seen it all before. "The Tommies were from something called the SAS – you military fellahs'll know all about that, I expect. Sabotage, spying and all that kind of nasty business behind the lines. Treacherous shiteheels. Slip a knife in between yer ribs without a frigging second thought. Anyway they'd been working with the Frogs, blowing up bridges, railway lines – the usual stuff and so we classified them as commandos." He paused and looked at von Thoma, standing at the head of the L-Squad, almost as if he were challenging him to say something. When von Thoma didn't, he said. "Of course you all know the Führer's Commando Order* and what it implies. So we didn't have to mess around with a frigging lot of mealy-mouthed, hair-splitting judges, advocates and the like. We made short work of 'em."

He gave the L-Squad his lopsided smile and crooked his right forefinger, pulling it back, as if drawing a trigger. "Right at the back of the skull. All over in zero, comma, nothing. Never felt a thing, I'd guess."

Von Thoma pulled a face. He could visualise the scene. The Tommies forced to kneel, wondering what was going to happen to them. The cold metal of a muzzle placed at the base of their skulls just behind the right ear. That sudden terrible overwhelming realisation that their life was now going to end suddenly, violently – and that there was nothing they could do about it.

"So that's how you got your uniforms, courtesy nice old *Oberkommissar* Hart—"

Skorzeny cut the self-satisfied cop short with a brisk "Thank you, Hartwig, but time is running out. We, here, have a lot to get through this day. Perhaps you'd fill my people in with the details of this SAS unit and then hand out what identification you took off them. Thank you."

The fat Gestapo cop looked peeved, but he obviously realised that even the feared name of the Gestapo pulled no weight with the Führer's new favourite, Skorzeny, the 'hero' who had rescued *il Duce*, so he got on with it to be dismissed a few minutes later with, "You'll find beer and salami in the NCO mess kitchen, *Oberkommissar*." He wasn't even being allowed the good real bean coffee, enjoyed by these special

---

* Hitler's 1942 'Commando Order', stated that anyone found behind the lines in the Reich and Occupied Territories, even if he was in uniform, could be shot without trial.

troops* in the officers" mess. Sullenly, not even attempting to salute the *Obersturmbannführer*, the Gestapo man left.

Skorzeny waited until he was out of earshot before saying, "So now you know the reason for the British uniforms and something about the methods of these English special troops. The next question, which must be puzzling you, is to what use you will put these uniforms and your new knowledge, eh?" He beamed at them like a benevolent uncle, though von Thoma thought that if he had ever had an uncle like that with his horrifically scarred face, he would probably have spent his childhood having nightmares.

"I shall tell you. But first you must know a little – as much as you need to know – of the Führer's strategy and plans for the next few weeks." He snapped his fingers and one of his elegantly uniformed SS adjutants came running, as if he had been waiting for this summons all morning, map board clasped under his arm.

Hurriedly he placed it on the waiting easel, saluted and stepped back, still remaining stiffly at attention. Skorzeny indicated with a wave of his big paw that they should break ranks and come closer. Nervously, and wondering what kind of rabbit the *Obersturmbannführer* was going to pull out of the hat now, they did so. As they moved in, von Thoma noted that the non-German-speaking SS guards, who had escorted them the first night, began to close in as well, almost as if they were sealing off the area. Later he realised that was exactly what they were doing.

Skorzeny slapped the map with his big paw. "The Belgian Ardennes is between here, Echternach in Luxembourg and Monschau, here in the north, in the Reich. Some ninety

---

* In wartime rationed Germany great distinction was made between *ersatzkaffee* made of acorns and the real stuff, an important treat for those who could obtain it.

kilometres of front in all, I should say." He paused and let the information sink in. But all of them were used to such briefings. How many fine plans had they heard over these last two or three years which would bring the war to a successful end for Germany, but which had all ended in failure? They were not impressed. Still curiosity got the better of them and they continued to listen for the ever-presence of those surly non-German speaking SS guards meant that no one was going to get out of this remote camp – if he didn't follow orders – *alive*.

Skorzeny obviously thought he had made the most of his dramatic pause. Now he snapped hastily, his breath fogging grey on the cold autumn air, as if he were glad to get the words off his broad chest, "Soon the Führer, in his great wisdom, intends to attack through that front. Undoubtedly he will catch the *Amis* by surprise." He waited until the excited murmuring and gasps of surprise had died down, before adding confidently, "Even if the Führer doesn't catch the enemy off guard, it won't matter. Our forces will outnumber the four *Ami* divisions stationed in that area by at least ten to one." He beamed at them with that sallow, scarred face of his. "Intelligence estimates the *Amis* number some eighty thousand men. We shall attack them with *three* armies – a total of nearly six hundred thousand German soldiers in all."

Even von Thoma was impressed. Where had the Reich found so many soldiers at this stage of the war? he asked himself in bewilderment. He thought Hitler was scraping the barrel. Now like some conjuror pulling a white rabbit out of his top hat to the delighted surprise of his audience, he had actually been able to form three new assault armies.

Skorzeny said, "My own brigade will take part in the great attack, but that, *Manner*, is of no concern to you. Your duties will lie elsewhere." He slapped the map once more with his hamlike fist. "To the south of the assault area in the Ardennes lie two *Ami* armies – General Patton's Third and beyond that – here in French Alsace, which you know the French stole from us after the First World War – General Hodges' Seventh."

Von Thoma groaned inwardly. This was no time, he told himself, for a lesson in ancient history, especially from an Austrian like Skorzeny. *'Get on with it, man,'* he urged silently.

Skorzeny seemed to read his mind and continued. "Now it is the Führer's main worry that the enemy leaders will order the US 7th Army – here in Alsace – to move up and take over the area now controlled by Patton's Third. Why?" Skorzeny answered his own question. "Because our Intelligence believes that the enemy, once he realises how serious the threat in the Ardennes is, will command this cowboy General Patton to attack into the flank of our assault armies. This cannot be allowed to occur. Our assault armies cannot afford to waste a single minute fending off a flank attack by the *Amis*. Time is of the essence. They must reach the Channel and split the British from the American armies. Then the Führer feels that the Anglo-American gangsters will grant Germany a more favourable peace than that of unconditional surrender.* The Reich will be saved and we can take care of the Ivans –" he meant the Russians "– on our eastern front in due course, while the Anglo-Americans sit back and watch them being destroyed . . . which, of course, is what they really want."

Skorzeny paused, as if he had done too much talking for a man of action such as he believed he was. He reached into the pocket of his breeches and, pulling out a silver flask took a hearty swig from it, while von Thoma's brain raced electrically, running over what he had just heard.

There was a crazy logic about Hitler's grandiose plan. The

* The Western Allies had demanded 'unconditional surrender' from the Germans the year before, which made it clear to thinking Germans that there was no hope for them; they would have to fight to the bitter end.

British, after five years of war, were about exhausted, von Thoma knew. They were running out of fighting men. They wouldn't survive another Dunkirk and without England as a base the Americans would be in a pickle. With a lot of luck on his side Hitler might just pull it off and achieve a respectable peace for the poor battered Reich and its long-suffering citizens.

"So," Skorzeny gasped, as if what he had just drunk had taken his breath away, "we must make sure that the US Third Army," he said the name scornfully with the typical contempt of the German for the American soldier, "doesn't do that." He fixed them with his hard, dark-eyed stare.

Von Thoma felt they had listened tamely too long. After all his neck was on the block obviously. He wanted to know what all this had to do with him and his new command – the L Squad, whatever that was supposed to signify. "*Obersturmbannführer?*" he called.

Skorzeny looked at him surprised. He was not used to being interrupted, that was obvious. "Yes?"

"May I ask what we have to do with these great plans? What role do you envisage for us . . . if we are not to take part in the main attack?"

"I am glad you asked that question, von Thoma," he answered with a smile, though it was clear he wasn't glad one bit. "But before I give you my full answer, there is one task you must carry out with your L-Squad."

"It is, *Obersturmbannführer?*"

Skorzeny allowed himself a careful smile. "We would like to try you out in your role of SAS soldiers. We are hoping that the *Amis* will never have heard of this formation. Even if they have, they will attribute your different accent in the English language to your being English. The English, as you know, do not speak the American dialect."

Von Thoma flushed impatiently. He didn't want a lecture

on the English language from a man who probably only spoke a couple of words of the tongue himself and had never visited the island kingdom in all his life. "And then?" he rasped in that harsh Prussian manner of his: the tone of a man used to issuing orders and having them obeyed."

"And then, *mein lieb Herr von Thoma*, after you have successfully completed the first stage of our great plan, you will be told your assignment. And, –" his voice rose as if he were addressing a rally of Party bully boys rather than a handful of shabby undernourished 'front swine', who lived their brutal violent lives from one day to the next "– I shall tell of the great mission that has been planned for you and your Lethal Squad."

The words cut through von Thoma like a razor-sharp knife. *Lethal Squad*! So that was it! Now he knew instinctively he and his men hadn't a chance in hell of surviving what was to come.

Four

"*Was um Himmelswillen –*" Skorzeny exploded, as the door to his office was flung open and the big tough Berliner from the L-Squad staggered in, bearing a huge can with American lettering on it, plus a box tucked under his right arm, as if it were some kid's toy. The Berliner smiled, shifted the looted *Ami* cigar from one side of his mouth to the other and said, "Permission to report, *Obersturmbannführer.*"

"What in three devils" name is going on—" Skorzeny began again, half rising from his seat, face indignant. But once more he was interrupted by von Thoma who now entered, also bearing a similar packing case to the Berliner. "Loot," he announced, apropos of nothing. "Thought the gentlemen of the staff," the harshly handsome young officer could barely restrain his sneer, "would like to share the spoils."

"Spoils?"

"*Jawohl, ja.*" Von Thoma pulled the carton of looted *Camels* from the back of his webbing belt and slung them carelessly on the desk, "Cigarettes, *Obersturmbannführer. Ami Camels.* Much better than the real camel shit your poor, hairy-assed stubble hopper has to smoke in the Army."

Skorzeny looked at the two of them severely. "Are you drunk?" he snapped.

Vom Thoma wasn't put out one bit. He no longer cared after the run-in with the Americans near Metz. What could Skorzeny do to him worse than the *Amis* had tried to do? He could only

88

shoot him. "A bit," he admitted. "We would have brought some of the *Ami* firewater for you, but that big ape over there," he indicated a grinning Schulze, who tugged at the end of his big red nose, as if in embarrassment, "slipped most of it behind his collar while we were sleeping last night."

"For medical reasons, sir, I can assure you," Schulze answered.

But von Thoma ignored him now. He wanted to know the truth. That business with the *Amis* had been very hairy and he hadn't liked recce-ing that French road to Nancy one bit. If he was going to carry out a mission for Folk, Fatherland and Führer, he wanted to know what the odds were. So without wasting any further time, he said straight out, "All right, *Obersturmbannführer* – an Ascension Day commando, eh?"* He waited, suddenly nervous, realising he didn't want to die – just like that.

Skorzeny took his time. He was back in charge once more. Finally, he said with a little shrug, "I hope not . . . I sincerely do."

Von Thoma clicked his tongue impatiently.

Skorzeny gave him what he wanted to know – and it wasn't good. "The Führer," he intoned, "commanded that the L-Squad is to carry out a task of the utmost importance to the success of the great offensive—"

"Kill Patton," von Thoma beat him to it, knowing he had been half aware of the truth ever since Skorzeny had lectured them the week before on the coming offensive in the West.

"Exactly," Skorzeny agreed. "The American Cowboy General must die." He coughed delicately, as if suddenly he was oddly embarrassed. "Yes, that is what it's all about."

Next to an abruptly white-faced von Thoma, Schulze crossed himself with mock piety, intoning in a sepulchral voice, "For what we are about to receive, let the Good Lord make us truly shitting thankful . . ."

* A one-way trip to heaven – or hell! i.e. mission without a return.

Five

"Pass the word back," Savage whispered to Hairless Hairy, who was just behind him, "we dump the Frogs soon." He flashed a look up at the handful of French civilians up front, working their way through the slagheaps and broken, rusty bogies once used in the mines of the area, which Pepé said marked the extent of the German perimeter around Metz. They had not noticed anything.

"Dump, Major?" Hairless queried *sotto voce*.

"Yeah." Savage drew his finger across his throat. "This way if necessary."

"Got ya, Major. Couldn't happen to a nicer set of guys." Barely turning his big hairless head, he whispered out of the side of his mouth like some mobster in a Hollywood crime movie, "Gonna dump the Frogs when the major gives the word. Git it . . . pass it on . . ."

They had been going for over two hours now with the light going all the time. In an hour or so, Savage guessed it would be dark; darkness came early in this sombre war-torn valley in which the great fortress city of Metz was set. But he was glad of the impending darkness. It would provide the cover they would need and any help that Nature could give them would be gratefully received, the Ranger major told himself grimly.

So far, however, the French had done everything expected of them. They had smuggled the little band of bold Rangers past a German forward-listening post easily, skirting the

90

minefield which surrounded the place and vanishing into the shattered pines beyond, heading for the industrial district of Mazières-les-Metz. If they were going to betray his Rangers to the Krauts, Savage wondered, puzzled, why not do it there and then? Why risk the inherent dangers that lay in every square yard of German-held territory. All the same, Savage knew in his bones, as if it were some God-given truth, that the runtish French leader they called Pepé would betray them at the drop of a hat as soon as it scrvcd his purpose to do so. When that would be, Savage didn't know. All he knew was that he'd have to beat the traitor 'to the draw', as the Texan-born Hairless Harry would have put it in that slow drawl of his, before spitting drily into the dust.

Time passed. But although the front was quietening as though preparing for the long cold night ahead, with the guns almost silent now, Savage could feel the tension almost physically. Over and over again, he had to resist the temptation to look behind him, half suspecting they were being followed across this lunar landscape. Once he felt the small hairs at the back of his skull grow erect, as he heard something shuffling through the skeletal undergrowth to their right. Instinctively, he grabbed for the safety of his carbine, heart thumping away like a crazy trip-hammer. A moment later he gave a gasp of heartfelt relief, as a cow emerged clumsily, her udder swollen with milk.

"Christ on a Crutch," Hairless Harry breathed, "I nearly pissed myself!"

"What d'ya mean – *nearly*," the next Ranger in the file behind him moaned. "I *did*!"

"Knock it off," Savage hissed urgently, but he had difficulty in recognising his own voice as he did so.

Five minutes later or thereabouts, Pepé raised his right hand, not taking his gaze off the darkening horizon. It was the signal to halt. "Okay, guys, keep yer eyes skinned."

"Like canned tomatoes," Hairless Harry whispered in an attempt at humour. No one laughed.

Crouched low, carbine at the ready, Savage hurried forward to where Pepé bent at the head of his Frenchmen. "What's the drill?" he asked urgently.

"Drill?" Pepé ignored the word he obviously couldn't understand and said instead, "Soon we leave. You see that chimney." He indicated the shattered chimney of an abandoned, shell-pocked nineteenth-century factory to the right. "It is the main line of the Boche. They had soldiers there. But to the left . . . You see that wood?"

Again Savage nodded. He had already spotted the wood, most of its trees shattered and broken off by the shellfire like a bunch of matchsticks. "Yes."

"That wood is empty. The Boche, they used it before for – what's the word, *coar*"

"Latrines?" Savage ventured.

"Yes. Latrines. Now they stay in the factory. *Les Salauds*. They are filthy – the Boche." He pulled a face.

Yeah, a hard little voice at the back of Savage's head rasped, but their dough isn't. Aloud he said, "You want us to use that wood to infiltrate their MLR – er – main line of resistance."

"Yes, *Bien sûr*," Pepé agreed, but Savage noted instantly that the Frenchman kept his shifty gaze on the ground, as if he didn't want the American to see the look in his eyes in the growing darkness. But Savage didn't need to. He knew instinctively this was the trap. Casually he said, not betraying his suspicions for one moment, "And you . . . what will you do, Pepé?" Now it was his turn to keep his gaze lowered.

"I shall return," the Frenchman answered hesitantly. "I have business with the nigger you know."

Savage told himself that Whitey, with that enormous chip on his shoulder due to his colour, would have gladly slaughtered the Frenchman personally if he had been able to hear that derogatory description. "And after we pass through?" Savage ventured, as if he hadn't heard the word.

"I have the address ready," Pepé said immediately. "It is on the outskirts of Mazières." He fumbled in the pocket of his leather waistcoat. "It is a *maison de passe*." To make his meaning quite clear, he thrust the forefinger of his right hand back and forth rapidly into a circle formed by the thumb and index finger of his other hand.

"A cathouse," Savage said hastily. "You want us to contact someone in the cathouse. They will give us further instructions?"

"*Oui* . . . cathouse."

"They can be trusted?"

"Yes . . . yes . . . now you must go. No time for talk." He thrust the folded slip of paper into Savage's hand hastily and made a shooing gesture in the French style which indicated they should leave at once.

Savage hesitated. Now that the time had come to deal with Pepé and his rogues, he couldn't bring himself to do it. He couldn't slaughter them in cold blood; it went against all the traditions in which he had been brought up. It was the greatest inhibition that had faced the average American GI from the very start in the Army: how did you make a guy kill some unknown fellow human being without a second thought?

Hairless Harry seemingly had no such inhibitions. Perhaps he still had the blood of his lawless Texan forefathers who, in the frontier tradition, shot first and asked questions afterwards. He rose to his feet, finger on the trigger of his tommy gun. "Run for it guys," he yelled, startling the other Rangers. "Them trees at two o'clock *MOVE!*" Hairless Harry didn't wait to check whether they were following his command. Instead he pointed the big, powerful Thompson at the battered factory, which the Germans held, and pulled the trigger.

"NO—" The rest of Savage's words were drowned in the

heavy frenetic chatter of the sub-machine gun. Through the air
.45 slugs hissed lethally. Brick dust erupted the length of the
factory wall. For a moment the totally surprised French were
frozen in mid-stride. Not the Rangers. They knew the balloon
was about to go up. There was no time for second thoughts.
With Savage in the lead, they blundered through their guides
and pelted for the cover of the woods. In that very same instant
there came the high-pitched, hysterical hiss of a Spandau from
the factory. White tracer sliced the air. It zipped towards the
spot where the Rangers had been a moment before. But they
had vanished already. Instead the French took the full lethal
impact of that first terrible burst. They were whirled round and
round like puppets in the hands of some fiendish puppet-master
who had suddenly gone mad. They fell screaming with agony,
blood jetting in scarlet arcs from their wounds. Desperately
Pepé tried to remain upright. His clawlike hands clutched the
air like those of a man ascending the rungs of an invisible
ladder. Strange, guttural sounds came from deep down within
the dying Frenchman, as blood spurted from the line of red
buttonholes suddenly stitched the length of his skinny chest.
He was fighting to remain upright. Like some boxer refusing to
go down for a count of ten. To no avail! Abruptly he gave a low
despairing groan. Slowly his legs started to collapse beneath
him. The German machine gunner swung his terrible weapon
round once more. A thousand bullets a minute poured from its
narrow, air-cooled muzzle. Pepé was torn apart. Huge gory
pieces of his shattered flesh flew everywhere. He disappeared
in a welter of blood in the very same moment that a gasping
Savage cried, "Keep moving, guys . . . keep moving for God's
sake—" And then, too, they were gone, leaving the sound of the
firing behind them, echoing and re-echoing around the circle
of hills as if it would never end . . .

It was a night of alarms and excursions. Hairless Harry had

certainly dealt with the French, who obviously would have betrayed them sooner or later, but equally obviously that sudden burst of sub-machine gun fire had alerted the whole of the front north of Metz. "Perhaps the Frogs squealed," Savage had gasped, chest heaving with his efforts, face lathered with sweat, despite the night cold. "Perhaps it was the tommy gun . . . I don't know – or care. All I know is that they know where we—" He never finished his explanation, for again the star shells were bursting high over their heads in spurts of icy silver and again they could hear the fierce baying of bloodhounds in the far distance. The Krauts were on the trail again. They broke cover and once again ran for a fresh hiding place.

Thus it had been for the last three hours or so. Now it was well past midnight and still the Germans continued to hunt them. "They're very persistent people, aren't they?" young Peover, the scion of a rich New England family which had come over with the *Mayflower* and at nineteen the youngest member of the Ranger Squad said. "Never give up, do they?"

"I'd give them 'giving up'," Hairless Harry growled threateningly, "if I had my way, I'd saw the nuts off'n every goddam one of them Heinies – with a blunt razor blade!" He spat as was customary.

Savage ignored the dire threat. "Listen guys," he said, eyeing the star shells, which coloured their upturned faces in a sparkling unnatural hue, "we've got to get under cover. Sooner or later they're gonna stumble across us, especially when it gets light."

Numbly the others, almost exhausted by now, nodded their agreement. "But where, sir?" Peover, the product of Groton and a freshman year at Yale, asked a little plaintively.

"Ever been inside a cathouse, Peover?" Savage asked, knowing the teenager, who blushed constantly at the slightest provocation, hadn't.

Hairless Harry guffawed coarsely and said, "Hell, sir,

Pissover here, wouldn't be able to find his way into a whore's cot, even if she signposted it and walkie-talked him in personally."

Peover blushed predictably and said in a low voice. "No sir. I don't think Mamma would approve. Not done."

The exhausted men laughed softly and Savage felt sorry for the kid; he was always taking a lot of stick from the other Joes. "Well, Peover this morning you're going to enjoy that experience for the very first time."

"But Major," Hairless Harry objected swiftly, "how do we know we can trust them Frogs, even if they do work in a cathouse?"

"The short answer, Sergeant, is we can't. But what alternative—" He never completed his sentence, for in that instant a harsh voice proclaimed *"Hey da, was macht ihr?"* The Rangers didn't wait for any further questions to come hurtling their way. Instead they were running again, their exhaustion vanished, going all out, as if the Devil himself were at their heels. Which, in a way, he was.

Six

"*Holy cow.*" Pfc Peover gasped, voice full of awe, as he peered in through the slit in the eighteenth-century house's shutter. "*Wow . . . golly jeepers!*"

"What is it, Pissover?" Hairless Harry hissed urgently, as he balanced the young innocent on his wrestler's shoulders.

Next to him in the small perimeter formed automatically by the Rangers around the silent 'cathouse', Major Savage bit his lip anxiously. So far they had managed to evade the enemy. But he knew their luck would run out sooner or later. Already as they had crept into the shattered little industrial town of Mazières-les-Metz they had just dodged a German patrol by the skin of their teeth; and in the distance he could hear the steady nailed tread of yet another on the glistening white *pavé* of the place. Understandably, this close to the front, the Krauts weren't taking any chances, especially as they knew by now of the presence of his little force of Rangers behind their lines.

Balancing awkwardly on Hairless's shoulders, Peover gave another shocked gasp and muttered, as if to himself, "I simply just don't believe it . . . I simply don't!"

"What the frigging Sam Hill don't ya believe?" Hairless Harry snarled, running out of patience fast. "C'mon baby, shoot it to me."

But at that particular moment, young Peover wasn't 'shooting' answers to anyone. He was too intrigued with what he was watching on the other side of the dirty bedroom windowpane.

Until he had joined the Rangers straight from that upper-class expensive Ivy League college of his, he had led a very sheltered life. Even in the sexually uninhibited Rangers he had never seen anything quite like this, even at the *'exhibitions'* that his comrades-in-arms had dragged him to near the Place Pigalle – 'Pig Alley' – in Paris. He was savouring every second of it now; it would be something for his memoirs, he told himself. Yeah, a little voice inside his head sneered, if you live that long, shitehawk!

An enormously fat whore lay in the centre of a sagging brass bed like a stranded whale. She was dressed in black stays, wore knee-length black boots with enormous spiked heels that would undoubtedly buckle beneath her once she brought her full weight to bear on them when she stood up. Why, a gaping-mouthed Peover told himself, one of her enormous dugs alone had to weigh at least ten pounds.

But that wasn't the end of it. Crouched at her feet was an equally fat man, also naked, his pince-nez, balanced on his sweat-lathered nose, steamed up as he worked all-out on her boots. He was polishing them furiously, as if his very life depended upon it, with the fat whore wielding a black lash, flicking it across his pudgy back every time he seemed about to slacken in his efforts with his brushes and polishing rags. And all the while the naked man, gasped furiously as if he might have an heart attack at any moment, whispering whenever he had the breath to do so, *"Ach, die Schande . . . die Schande . . ."**

Not that the fat whore seemed one bit worried about the state of the strange German's health. She flicked her whip without thought or intent, staring in a bored fashion at the flaking, dirty ceiling above the bed, as if she was count- ing the pieces of plaster that came floating down every

* The shame . . . the shame of it all.

time they were dislodged by the sweaty efforts of the man below.

"*Peover*." It was Major Savage. His voice sounded irate and at the same time jumpy.

Peover realised he couldn't waste any more of the Major's precious time enjoying the strange sexual scene taking place in this remote French township in the middle of the night; though the enormous fat whore had just idly flicked her lash across the man's naked rump and raised an immediate scarlet weal, which occasioned him to moan with delight and renew his efforts at polishing. He dropped lightly and Hairless Harry grunted, surly as ever, "Bout frigging time."

"'Kay, Peover, what's going on up there?" Savage asked swiftly, noting as he asked that the *maison de passe* was absolutely silent, as if the whore above them was the only one still in business on her back. "What gives?"

Hurriedly Peover explained what he had just seen. Above them the old brass bed was beginning to squeak merrily now and there was the sound of excited panting. A high-pitched voice was gasping in German, "*Ich spritze . . . Heilig Stroksack, ich spritze, Mensch!*"

On any other occasion Savage would have been inclined to laugh at the scene. But not now. Time was running out. The steady tread of the German patrol was getting closer. Now he had to make a quick decision, based, in part, on what Peover had seen, whether he could entrust his Rangers to the supposed kind hearts of the local whores. And there ain't no such thing as a kind-hearted whore, he told himself, using the tone that Hairless Harry might have employed. They've got cash registers for hearts, broads like that.

But Savage, as he listened to what Peover had to report, knew he couldn't afford to be finicky. The heavy tramp was already in the next street. In a matter of moments the German patrol would turn the corner and they would be spotted, "'Kay," he snapped, as up above the hectic squeaking came to an abrupt halt, followed by a sudden and profound silence, "we're going in, guys."

Hairless Harry had heard the patrol too. He rasped. "Back or front, sir?"

"Back. Let's go . . ."

Moments later like grey predatory timber wolves they had melted into the silver darkness in the same instant that the heavy-footed patrol of 'chaindogs',* their badges of office around their necks gleaming, hove into view to find an empty street in front of them . . .

Petra *die Peitsche*,¶ as she was known to that small influential circle of French businessmen and German senior officers in Metz, was an angry woman; and when the enormously fat whore was angry, her clients and any other male who crossed her for that matter had better look out.

As she now snorted at *Standartenführer der Allgemeinen SS* Gross, head of Metz Garrison's security services, "Here am I, a poor weak woman, totally defenceless against you male swine," she raised a finger like a hairy pork sausage to her eye, as if to brush away a tear at the thought of just how defenceless she was, "who has sacrificed her all for you, worn her poor weak body to a frazzle in the service of the Reich. And what do I get for it? What can I expect now?" She threw out her plump, powdered hand expressively and her big white breasts trembled like jellies inside the tight confines of her black leather bra as if they might pop out at any moment and strike the *Standartenführer* a telling blow on the end of his pinched nose.

* German military policemen, so named on account of the silver crescents, held by a chain, suspended around their necks.
¶ Petra the Whip.

He moved back hastily, crying, "My dear Petra . . . Oh, please, Petra dear, don't excite yourself – *please!*"

Petra *die Peitsche* sniffed. "Typical man," she said. "Just want to soothe a poor weak woman so that you can have your wicked way with my pain-racked body once more."

"No, no," the German SS officer protested vehemently. "I wouldn't do such a thing. You know how much I love you and – er," he lowered his gaze delicately for a moment, "your boots."

"The *whip*! you mean," she growled suddenly, her old aggressive threatening self for an instant.

He shuddered with delicious anticipation.

But the fun and games were over for this night. For Petra was too much concerned with her own precious hide to be bothered tanning his. "What is to happen to me when you go back to the Reich?" she exclaimed plaintively. "So far we have played little games to amuse you. But what kind of *real* games do you think those supposed patriots would play with me once they have captured Metz, eh?"

"You needn't worry," Gross reassured her hurriedly. "I shall take care of you, rest assured of that."

"How?" she sneered. "Metz is surrounded. Do we fly out? What shall we live on when you're a poor slob of a petty farmer, for mark me, the Americans will turn the Reich into one great tenant farm – they've promised that, that Jew Morgenthau* of theirs. Anyway, the Reds here will have probably castrated you before then. They do it to all the SS."

"Do you think they might," he thrilled, suddenly interested despite her threats of woe and black tidings.

She ignored the remark. "Something must be done," she

---

* The US Secretary of State for Agriculture who had urged the US President to transform a beaten Nazi Germany into an eighteenth-century tenant-farming community.

announced with an air of finality, as if she had just made up her mind at last. *"Definitely*, something must be done. After all, I want to continue my profession long enough to save for my retirement."

"My little cheetah," Gross exclaimed and moved a little closer, gaze full of all that white flesh that overflowed her sparse black clothing like a melting ice pudding. "I shall take care of you."

She pushed him away with the end of her delightful whip. "Don't maul the goods with those fat porkies of yours until you explain," she threatened in her most intimidating voice.

"I think you worry too much," he began hesitantly, listening to the tramp of the *Feldgendarmerie* outside. "I have plans . . . the Führer plans—"

"Fuck the Füh—" Petra *die Peitsche* began, but stopped abruptly. In her many years as a *grande horizontale* she had learned that a working woman could earn more by keeping her mouth shut and her ears open – in more ways than one. So instead of insulting the German leader, who everyone knew possessed only one ball, which had caused all the trouble in the first place, she said instead, "What exactly do you mean, my dear *Standartenführer?*"

Carefully Gross looked to left and right – 'the German look', as it was called – as if the Gestapo was standing behind the very door, then satisfied he wasn't being overheard, he said in a low voice, "Things are not so black as they might seem."

She nodded encouragingly, but said nothing.

"The Führer has no intention of allowing those decadent Anglo-Americans to overrun our beloved Germany. Indeed the boot will be on the other foot. It is we Germans who will do the overrunning. The war is not lost by the Reich by a long chalk. We have our military intentions—"

"You mean an attack?"

He beamed at her sudden enthusiasm and change of mood.

"I knew that would make you happy, sweet little woman," he simpered and looked at the cruel black lash a little hopefully.

Petra had other things on her mind than slap and tickle. She rapped swiffly. "Will there be money in it?"

"*Naturlich*. There's always loot in an offensive, Petra," he answered. "I can see you now. All piccobello in black – velvet naturally – with, dare I say it? – a new whip. A real cruel one with—"

It was then that it had happened and suddenly, as the body came flying in, or so it seemed, and Petra screamed (as much as that tough old *grande horizontale* was ever capable of such an utterance). *Standartenführer* Otto Gross felt everything turn black in front of his eyes and that 'really cruel whip' vanished as irretrievably as do all of life's great illusions . . .

Seven

C olonel Charles Codman, Patton's aide, was puzzled.
Despite the fact that his chief hated his current task, he could see that behind Patton's solemn, grave face, he was excited, even happy. But why? On the face of it the Commander of the US 3rd Army had nothing to be happy about as he stood there at the side of the road, waiting for each of the boxlike ambulances to stop momentarily, while he spoke a few words to the wounded they carried.

Every man received a Purple Heart, pinned on personally by the three-star general, even the old soldier who confessed, "I ain't really wounded, General. I've just got a case of them bleeding piles." To which Patton had replied, without a flicker of humour crossing his serious face, "Son, whatever you've got, you've shed your blood for the United States of America. You deserve your medal just like the rest." And with that Patton had pinned the medal for having been wounded on the puzzled soldier's 'Ike' jacket.

On any other occasion, Codman would have permitted himself a little smirk at the soldier's confession and Patton's reply. But not this grey November morning, he was too confused.

While Patton waited for news from Major Savage's lost patrol of Rangers, he had ordered a battalion-strength attack yet again on Metz's fortifications. As he had explained it to his staff late the previous night back in Nancy, "I know gentlemen, it's throwing good money after bad. We haven't got a chance in hell of forcing those goddam Boche fortifications from the front." He had paused and made them wait for the punch line. It was an old rhetorical habit of his and one that had helped to make Patton such good copy among the war correspondents. Old Blood an' Guts was always good for a damned fine quote. "But unfortunately we're gonna have to sacrifice a damned fine infantry battalion tomorrow morning in yet another frontal attack. We've got to convince the Krauts we haven't got anything else up our sleeves. We've played all our aces."

There were sombre nods of agreement from the assembled colonels and generals. It was all part and parcel of the grand strategy, they obviously told themselves. The cost in human misery and lives had nothing to do with them. That was the lot of younger men. *They*'d probably die in a nice, comfortable bed of old age.

"Later in the day when the fields are no longer locked in with the usual goddam morning fog here in Lorraine, our ships'll go and give Metz another pounding from the sky. That, too, will fit in with the Heinies" concept of our tactics. But by then, gentlemen, Savage will have – I hope – found the back door into Fort Driant. Then as the GIs say, *we'll really start cooking with gas!*" It had been the punchline which had signalled the end of the conference.

Now the fresh battalion attack had failed as Patton had expected it would. The survivors were streaming back, wild or blank looks in their eyes, some so shocked by their ordeal that they didn't even recognise Patton. A few without their weapons. An officer, blood-stained bandage around his head under his helmet, muttering to himself, his whole skinny body twitching compulsively at regular intervals. But even that particular sight didn't seem to spoil Patton's mood, Codman noted. Under normal circumstances, the boss would have chewed the shell-shocked officer out, perhaps even slapped him and threatened him with a firing squad as 'a goddam yellow coward'. Now, instead, the Third Army Commander said mildly, "It'll be okay, son. Just you go on back. The medics'll fix you up good . . . It'll be okay." And he had smiled as the young shavetail looey had staggered off down the shell-pitted road to the rear.

Finally Patton felt he had done enough as an Army Commander. "The troops have been rallied, Codman," he said, pleasantly enough for him, though the usual scowl had returned to his face; it was, of course, part and parcel of his 'war face', the one he practised in front of the mirror in his bedroom at night. "What of Savage?"

"Nothing as yet, sir," Codman replied promptly, watching some blacks of the Graves Commision scooping up the bits and pieces of an unfortunate GI who had been hit by a mortar bomb. One of them, whistling tonelessly, was carrying the man's head, complete with helmet, towards their 'deuce-and-a-half' truck in a bucket, which dripped blood into the mud behind him. "But they're not due on air till twelve hundred hours, sir."

Patton nodded his understanding casually and said, "'Kay, we'll let the fly-boys have go at Metz. But Codman, make sure that they don't drop more than a couple of token two hundred and fifty pounders in the Mezières-les-Metz area. I don't want Savage to have more problems than necessary."

"Wilco sir." Codman frowned. "But if we hit Metz again, the French will suffer."

Patton shrugged carelessly. "The Frogs should have thought of that when they let themselves be trapped inside Metz with the Krauts. You know, Codman," he added in a lowered voice. "These years in Europe since 1942 have simply reinforced my prejudices."

"Now do you mean, sir?"

"Well, look at the Arabs we met in North Africa way back then. Not a pot to piss in and no ambition to earn the price of

one – not like your average American. The Kikes we've met –
they know how to make dough, of course." He sniggered. "But
our Hebrew brethren are like that all over the world. The Limeys," he shrugged expressively, "well what can ya say about
them and that little fart of theirs, Monty, that's new – or com-
plimentary? So we come to the Frogs. Their dames are okay
in the sack." He chuckled at the memory. "I remember that well
from the old war and Gay Paree. Otherwise –" He paused, as if
he was thinking hard, "Come to think of it, the only Europeans
I've got much respect for are the Krauts. At least, they make
damned fine soldiers, eh, Codman?" He looked hard at his aide.

Codman lowered his gaze and thought it wiser not to speak.
He wondered, all the same, what the folks back home would
make of a statement like that: an army commander who thought
the enemy was superior to the most important ally, the British.

Codman dismissed the thought. "Orders, sir?" he snapped,
trying not to look at the 'darkies' as they attempted to thrust
shovefuls of human offal into a body bag made out of a mattress
cover and not succeeding, "Where now?"

"Back to Nancy. If I give out any more Purple Hearts like
this, I'll need one myself for a twisted wrist. Home James and
don't spare the horses. Let's see what Major Savage and his
merry men have to report . . ."

It had been Petra *die Peitsche*'s idea, aided by Peover, whose
youthful good looks and smattering of college French had
obviously made an impression on that gross, overripe female
with her suspicion of a black moustache. Indeed she had
reacted with surprising speed to the new situation as Hairless
Harry had come barrelling through the window, sending the
Standartenführer reeling back into the corner of her bedroom.
"*Lass" ihn nicht entkommen!*" she had bellowed in her basso
profundo. "Don't let him escape. *Il est très important.*"

In the event *Standartenführer* Gross, who was apparently so '*très important*', had not the slightest intention of getting away. He had been caught by complete surprise and had been totally winded by the human thunderbolt which had erupted through the window of the brothel so abruptly. Instead he lay, gasping frantically for breath, like a stranded whale.

Not Petra. She had recognised the American uniforms immediately and slipped into her new role of a latterday Jeanne d'Arc, rescued from the fiendish Boche, at once. Wringing her hands above her head, as if she were delivering her heartfelt thanks to '*le bon Dieu*' personally, she cried in Lorraine German, "My saviours . . . just in time", reaching out for a red-faced Peover who had followed Harry through the shattered window with a hand like a small steam shovel. Naturally Peover, being Peover, had backed off immediately, leaving Hairless Harry to comment in awe, "Holy shit, all that meat and no potatoes!" He had licked his lips, as if he could already visualise the enormous whore spread-eagled naked on a great platter just ready for consumption.

But that wasn't to be.

Hastily Petra explained who she was and who had been her 'client' – '*professional client*', as she had added delicately, as if that made all the difference. Asking to see Major Savage privately for a few moments, she had explained further that the *Standartenführer* seemed to know something very secret and very special. What that was exactly, she had not learned. But she did know that the German had promised her that things were going to change dramatically in Germany's favour on the Western Front.

Savage had been intrigued. But he realised that the brothel, especially now as its most prominent client *Standartenführer* Gross was missing, would not be the safest place in which to hide out until they were ready to carry out the rest of the plan. They'd have to find another hiding place. Indeed as they stood there, wondering what to do next, they could already hear angry cries and shouts of alarm as if someone had already tumbled to the fact that something was wrong.

Then Petra had come up with her surprising suggestion. "The railway yards," she had cried urgently, as the sound of running feet grew ever louder.

"Railroad yards?" Savage had echoed a little stupidly.

"Yes. Let that nice young man help me with my – er – things." She had looked pointedly at a still blushing Peover. "And I will show you."

The stench had been appalling. It was as if all the sewers and privies of the world had been opened. The stink hit the furtive little group sneaking its way through the bomb-shattered railway yard an almost physical blow. Hairless Harry, following Petra and Major Savage, his tommy gun at the ready, gasped and exclaimed, "Christ on a crutch. What a smell! I'll bring up my cookies in a second."

Savage, eyeing the shattered, twisted locomotives and the flat cars tipped to one side by the bomb explosions as if some naughty kid had overturned his toys, ignored the comment. Instead he whispered to Petra, who towered above him. "What are we looking for? Where's this hiding place?"

She raised her fat fingers to her carmine-coloured lips in a conspiratorial gesture and pointed to another long row of carriages to her right. "There," she whispered in German. "The Death Train."

"What?" Savage began, but Hairless Harry beat him to it. "Holy shit, Major," he exclaimed. "Look at them caskets! The train's full o' stiffs." He blanched in the grey morning gloom.

Petra hadn't understood the English, but obviously she had the intent. She smiled carefully and tapped the nearest coffin with her knuckles. There was a hollow sound. "Empty," she said.

Savage looked at her puzzled. "Empty?" he echoed. "So where in God Almighty is that horrible stink coming from then, eh?"

She smiled again at his bewilderment. Curling a big finger at them, she ordered with a wink at a still embarrassed Pfc Peover, "Follow me."

A couple of minutes later they had found the source of the nauseating stench. A freight car, full of cabbage had been hit. Its wooden staves had buckled with the impact to release its contents. Everywhere there were heads of yellow cabbages stinking to high heaven, with a yellow liquid oozing from them an inch deep.

Savage gulped hastily. He felt he was going to be sick. But he could understand why the fat whore had brought them to this awful place. "Here?" he queried, still hoping that this wasn't to be their hiding place.

She nodded and spread her arms across her massive bosom with an air of finality. "Here," she echoed.

Hairless Harry shook his bald head in mock despair. "Oh my aching frigging back, what a life!"

It was a sentiment that Savage could only echo. Reluctantly he started to help the others to pull away the front of the rotting stinking cabbages so that they could tunnel to the rear and their new hiding place; while Petra *die Peitsche* wagged her fat forefinger threateningly at a still bemused *Standartenführer* Gross, hissing at regular intervals, "One word from you, Boche, and it will be the whip."

"*Please*," was all that the fat SS officer could quaver in return . . .

Fifty miles away, in Nancy, Patton opened one eye and glanced at his bedside travelling clock. With pleasure he noted the date – Thursday, 2nd December 1944 – he gave one of his cold wintry smiles and said aloud, "Not long now." Then he turned over and went back to sleep easily, as if he hadn't a single care in the world.

PART III

It's easy to die for *nothing*, one should die for *something*.
General Patton

One

Cautiously, very cautiously, the lead jeep breasted the height. On both sides the skeletal trees were white and beautiful with their lacing of hoar-frost. Not that von Thoma, recently promoted to *Hauptman*, now uniformed as a captain in the British SAS, had eyes for the beauty of the winter landscape; he was too tense for that.

Instead, he indicated to the driver, he should pull over to the verge, behind the cover of the red-rusted German Mark IV tank, knocked out and abandoned by the retreating *Wehrmacht* three months before. The driver did so, gunning his engine in the winter cold, while von Thoma opened the flies of his thick serge khaki trousers and took a leak.

But the leak was only a cover. Von Thoma's eyes roamed the countryside around Verdun far down below and then across the River Meuse, snaking its way to the dead flat river plain beyond. Behind him he could hear the slow groan of the captured Humber armoured car working its way up the steep incline in low gear. He would have preferred an eight-wheel *Ami* 'Staghound' – they were faster and packed a more powerful punch – but Skorzeny had ordered the task force to use captured Tommy vehicles as much as possible and so he had to be content with the old-fashioned, less powerful, British armoured car.

Everything looked peaceful enough. There was steam or smoke coming from the US workshops to the right of the historic town next to the barracks but otherwise nothing seemed out of place. He had seen scores of such places in his time: soft billets behind the lines, where soldiers lived out their lives in relative comfort and no danger, the only threat that of catching a 'packet' – VD in some shape or form from the local *'Veronika Dankeschöns'*.*

He buttoned up his flies and casually, in case he was being observed, he swung his gaze to the crossroads far down below just outside the bridge which led into Verdun. As he had anticipated, there were guards there: GIs in khaki with their rifles slung over their shoulders, smoking in a fitful, bored manner, and middle-aged French gendarmes checking the civilians' *'cartes d'identité'*.

Von Thoma frowned. That way would be no good. Their papers wouldn't stand up to detailed scrutiny; nor would the English of his soldiers. One of the *Ami* sentries would inevitably spot the fake English-English. They'd have to find another route through Verdun on their way to Nancy, their final objective.

"Herr Hauptmann," Schulze sitting next to the driver, cradling a tommy gun across his knees, hissed. "Visitors – big brother to be exact."

Big brother! Von Thoma caught his breath. He knew the army slang expression only too well. It meant a tank. He swung round, trying to control his movement, but not succeeding too well. The noise of the Humber grinding up the steep incline to the heights, where the greatest battle in European history had been fought back in 1916 had drowned the clatter of the tank tracks. Now, almost upon them, was an *Ami* Sherman, stripped of the usual gear with which the tankers littered the decks of their armoured monsters, but with its gun intact and looking very formidable. Obviously the Sherman, newly painted and

* Soldiers' slang – 'Veronica thank yous', i.e. prostitutes.

114

with its tracks cleaned, had come from the workshops below and was returning to the front line outfit from which it had been sent for repairs. And it was all too clear that its commander, standing bolt upright in the Sherman's turret, was eyeing them with considerable interest.

It was understandable why. In their maroon berets and camouflaged Tommy smocks they stood out like a sore thumb in the middle of an American army corps.

Trying to look casual, von Thoma forced a toothy smile as the Sherman rolled ever closer, pretending at the same time that he was having difficulty doing up the stiff brass buttons of his flies. "Drop him, Schulze," he hissed out of the side of his mouth, smiling away all the time, "if the *Ami* bastard makes a wrong move."

"Don't worry, sir", the old hare answered. "The *Ami* sack-rat won't escape Frau Schulze's handsome son." Under cover of the windscreen, he pulled off his 'safety' and tensed over the sub-machine gun.

The seconds passed leadenly. To their right the old killing ground towered above them in brooding, ominous silence. Below, from the dull-silver snake of the Meuse, the stolid sound of hammering rose, blow upon blow. Von Thoma could feel the drops of cold sweat begin to start trickling down the small of his back unpleasantly. In a minute something would have to break, he knew that implicity. For the *Ami* tank commander was still staring at the stalled convoy of British vehicles, face revealing nothing but suspicion. Soon, von Thoma realised with the instant certainty of a a vision, the *Ami* was going to stop his Sherman and start asking awkward questions. Just in time he stopped himself for reaching for the English .38 revolver nestling in the green canvas holster at his side. That would have been a dead give-away.

Suddenly, startlingly, the Sherman's turret emitted a soft electric whirr. It began to turn slowly, but definitely. The big

75mm gun started to bear onto the little convoy. Von Thoma cursed. Had they been rumbled already? Perhaps not. All the same the tank commander was obviously suspicious. He was fiddling with his mike and saying something urgently over the intercom to the unseen driver below in his metal box.

Schulze's finger clutched the trigger of his tommy gun more firmly. Von Thoma's hand stole to the rear of his webbing belt and unhooked the grenade hanging there. Now the only sound was the furious beat of his own heart, thundering in his ears, and the grind of the Humber scout car lumbering painfully up the steep incline. Von Thoma resisted the desire to shout *fire*. After all that deadly 75mm and its co-axial machine gun would wipe them off the face of the earth, if they lost the draw.

Still von Thoma hesitated, although the Sherman's turret had come to a halt. Now the long cannon was pointing straight at his jeep. In the turret, the leather-helmeted *Ami* stood silently, threateningly. Why didn't he challenge? Why didn't he say something if he suspected they weren't all right? Still the Humber continued to grind its way up to that grim height, where once Germans and Frenchmen had slaughtered each other by the thousand, the hundred thousand and in the end by the million! Time seemed to have stopped. It was almost as if some God on high forbad them to desecrate this place of death yet again with further bloodshed.

Von Thoma clenched his teeth abruptly. Schulze shot him a glance. It was the moment of truth. He raised his tommy gun, jaw rigid, a nerve suddenly ticking out of control at his temple.

Von Thoma beat him to it. With one and the same movement he had unhooked, slipped out the cotter pin and hurled the little steel ball of a British grenade at the stationary tank.

Boom! It burst in a flash of violet angry light above the gun. The clang of steel striking steel. Next moment the *Ami* went sailing out of the turret, his severed hands still clutching its rim like red gloves. An instant later, Schulze joined in. Grinning wolfishly, he sprang to his feet in the jeep and pressed his trigger. "Try that fucker on for size!" he yelled savagely, as the tommy gun erupted at his right hip. Slugs riddled the front of the Sherman. They howled off like drops of heavy tropical rain on a tin roof. The driver, barely seen through his slit, reeled back. His face started to slip down from the bones like molten red wax. Next instant he had vanished and the rest of von Thoma's men were surging foreard, out of control, firing wildly, yelling like some battle-cry, "*Loot, boys . . . Ami loot . . .* !"

Schulze had volunteered to drag the shattered body of the faceless driver out of his leather and steel seat and drive the Sherman into the undergrowth, poor scrubby stuff that it was. For, even nearly three decades after the end of that terrible battle of the heights at Verdun, little grew on that accursed soil, soaked with the blood of two and a half million dead young men.

Now with their vehicles hidden in one of the seven abandoned villages of the battlefield, his subdued men enjoyed canned *Ami* coffee, while Schulze guzzled the bottle of looted bourbon which was his reward for having volunteered to remove that terrible corpse.

In the shattered stone around them, the young soldiers prepared for night, but without the usual noisy boisterousness of men relaxing in comparative safety. Instead they sat around the little blue-flickering fires of twigs and the like, cooking their evening meal – the normal block of concentrated peaflour to be turned into what they called 'fart soup', to be eaten with hunks of tinned black bread – in subdued silence.

"It's the place, sir," Schulze said, gasping pleasurably as he swallowed another tremendous slug of the looted booze, "Puts years on yer." He looked around at the scrubby trees and the ancient shell holes everywhere, white patched here and there with bones of those dead these many years.

"Suppose it is," von Thoma agreed, feeling subdued himself by the sombre atmosphere of that great killing ground of 1916. He cradled his hands around the metal canteen filled with steaming hot American coffee, as if suddenly chilled and heeding warmth. "Glad to be out of here in the morning." He shuddered.

Schulze forced a grin and tugged at the end of his great bulbous drinker's nose. "This place don't exactly fill yours truly with the joys o' life. All the same, sir, it's a good place to hide out. Who'd come up here to this arsehole of the world, in his right mind at this time of the night." He shivered dramatically and looked over his shoulder, as if he half expected some long dead Prussian Imperial Grenadier in his spiked helmet to come stealing out of the lengthening shadows.

"Exactly," von Thoma agreed and then raising his voice, changed the subject. "Stand-to at zero five hundred hours, Sergeant Schulze," he ordered in a businesslike manner, though he had never felt less like doing business, "just before first light."

"Right you are, sir. Will do."

"I've been looking at the map," von Thoma went on. "There's a side road that heads roughly south from the memorial site. Before the war the pilgrims—"

"Pilgrims?" Schulze interrupted the officer, puzzled.

"Yes, those who used to visit the graves of their loved ones killed in the battle, if they could find them. Anyway, pilgrims coming from the west and Paris would use it to avoid going through Verdun. Well, it has a side road that heads for Nancy, our objective. With a bit of luck, Schulze, we can be on it and heading for Patton's HQ there without being stopped by a roadblock check."

Schulze took a quick slug at his bottle and von Thoma watched enviously his Adam's apple going up and down his throat, as he swallowed the fiery brew. For the first time he felt he could use a stiff drink, too. Schulze coughed thickly and wiped the back of his big hand across his wet lips, saying, "That's all well and good. But once we reach Patton's HQ, how are we going to get inside without trouble? Place like that is bound to be well guarded. You know what our corps and army HQs are like. There are more guards and the like at such places than there are crabs in a sailor's pubic thatch."

Von Thoma laughed hollowly at the comparison. "I suppose you're right, Schulze, disgusting as the thought is. Naturally we've got faked documents but they'd be examined and that might cause trouble." He paused and looked at the broad honest face of his sergeant, outlined in the ruddy wavering light of the little fire. It was as if he were trying to see something there he had never seen before. Schulze shifted uneasily under such intense scrutiny and von Thoma relaxed his gaze hastily when he realised he was upsetting the NCO. "However, we do have a small ace up our sleeves, Schulze, you rogue," he said with feigned good humour.

"Ace, sir?"

"Yes, we have a contact inside Patton's HQ, who will help us. A sleeper, as Skorzeny calls them, planted there a long time ago."

Schulze's face lit up. "Now, sir, that *is* good news. But what kind of German could have managed to worm himself into Patton's HQ just like that."

Von Thoma took his time. "But this sleeper is *not* a German, at least not by birth." he explained, savouring the words slowly, anticipating the effect his words would have on the big NCO.

They did. "Not German!" he exclaimed.

"Yes," von Thoma answered easily, "and not one of your

locals who sided with the Reich when we were winning. All
those Frogs and Cheeseheads," he meant the Dutch, "who
thought the sun shone out of our arse in '40 and allowed
themselves to be bought later when they realised it didn't."

Schulze took a last swig of his bourbon before tucking
the precious bottle away for the night. "Yer, I know, *Herr
Hauptmann*. The worst kind of turncoat. Could do without
that kind."

"*Genau*. But this one is not like that. She's one of those
humble folk who fight on for our cause, although they know
what trouble the Reich is in because they believe in the New
Order that will save Europe and the rest of the world for that
matter— But you're not listening."

"I know sir," Schulze answered hesitantly. "Did you say
'*she*'?"

"I did," von Thoma answered, as if it were the most obvious
thing in the world that Skorzeny had a female spy in the heart
of the *Ami* Army Commander's HQ ready to risk her life for
the cause of the dying, defeated Reich.

Schulze whistled softly and as an afterthought took out his
bourbon and had another swig after all. "Some bit o' female
gash that one," he said in awe.

Von Thoma told himself that Schulze was right; she had to
be 'some bit o' female gash', as Schulze phrased it in his own
inimitable manner. He yawned on purpose. The conversation
had gone far enough; he had told Schulze too much already.
It was wiser to keep his mouth shut. "Better hit the hay," he
suggested.

"Right sir." Schulze drained his canteen, rolled his blanket
more tightly about his big body, murmured "*Traume suss*",*
chuckled and began snoring almost at once.

All around the men did the same. Now the only sound was

* Dream sweet.

that of the soft tread of the sentry and the faint hush of the wind in the tops of the winter trees. Von Thoma closed his eyes more firmly and willed himself to sleep. They were going to have an early start and undoubtedly a tough long day before them on the morrow. Metz was a mere sixty-nine kilometres from Verdun – an hour's drive at the most under normal circumstances. But tomorrow the circumstances would be anything but normal.

But all the same he couldn't get off to sleep. Instead he tossed and turned, his mind racing electrically, full of a hundred and one things. In the end, however, he drifted into an uneasy sleep, of frights and uncertainties. Above them on the heights, the first flakes of white began to filter out of the night sky and cover their still, blanketed bodies so that they would have appeared to any uninformed observer like men already dead, disappearing into the mantle of snow for ever . . .

Two

"*K*ikes . . . *Heebies* . . . go*ddam Moxies* . . ." the big WAC officer trembled with rage, her fat face flushed a bright searlet. "How dare that goddam Jew from New York ask *me* for my ID? God Almighty, doesn't he see me enter the goddam compound every frigging day that dawns." Angrily she slung her *Lucky Strike* at her feet and crushed it out with one of her outsize brogues.

The mild-mannered POL clerk, who usually had to bear the brunt of his superior's rages, which was often, said softly and soothingly, "Don't take it to heart, Major, Sergeant Weinstein was only doing his duty. It's been standard operating procedure since Monday."

Major Hartmann, head of HQ's POL* section and the COMZ¶ personal representative at Patton's Third Army HQ, lit another *Lucky* with her Zippo inhaling like a man before saying, "Cut out the crap, Jordan. Everyone and his brother at this HQ knows that goddam Yid has got it in for me ever since I said that Hitler wasn't altogether wrong when he treated the Jews the way he did. After all we didn't want them back in '40 in the States when they started coming across from Europe taking the jobs from our guys."

Pfc Jordan, who had always voted democrat ever since he

---

* Petrol and Oil supplies.
¶ Rear base area supply, with HQ located in Paris.

had been eligible to do so and had been known to give half a buck to the collectors from the National Association of Colored People in his time, kept his mouth shut although when he had been at college in New York he had had several Jewish friends.

Supreme Allied Headquarters was combing rearline outfits once again looking for riflemen reinforcements for the battered infantry divisions at the front and he knew that if he crossed Major Hartmann his name might well be on the next list of replacements. His liberal sentiments went only so far. He had no intention of throwing his life away for them. So he said, trying to change the subject, "Lots of new shipments of gas on the way from the port of Cherbourg, ma'am, and General Patton is squawking again that his armour is being stalled due to lack of gasoline. He's wanting to see you, ASAP."

Hartmann was not disconcerted by that summons to meet the commanding general 'as soon as possible – *damned possible*'. Patton was a man after her own heart: an American patriot who put the good ole U S of A first and hated these foreign Kikes who were trying to take over the States. "Did you get a time?"

"Just after this morning's briefing, ma'am," her clerk answered promptly, telling himself the big burly WAC major looked as if she might have graduated at college in freestyle wrestling. "Eleven hundred hours is my guess."

"Wilco," Hartmann snapped. "Excellent. 'Kay. Let's get this show on the road. I want to check a representative bunch of trip tickets. Just in case the commanding general asks how much juice we're losing to the Frog black market. You know those Kikes in the Service of Supply and those no-good damned Coloureds. They'd sell their own mothers to earn a fast buck."

"Yes ma'am," Pfc Jordan answered dutifully and hurried out to carry out her instructions, glad to get out of the female

Major's way for a time. One day, he knew, he'd flip if he were confined with her in the office too long and then he'd be up the line, having his nuts shot off by some hairy-assed Kraut. No, he couldn't chance that.

Hartmann waited till he had gone. Then she crossed the door, upon which was scrawled the old legend: THIS DOOR IS ALWAYS OPEN TO EVERYBODY. THE BUCK STOPS HERE. She closed it and satisfied she was alone, opened her desk drawer and took out the little pencilled sketch: the result of many hours of patient questioning, bribery and guesswork. It had been the real cause of her run-in with Sergeant Weinstein that morning, not the fact that he was Jewish.

Now, like one of her clerks secretly gloating over a pornographic magazine brought back from a seventy-two-hour furlough in Paris, she savoured what she had found out ever since 'they' had contacted her two weeks before. The route through the special entrance to the HQ compound in the *Rue Auxerre*, used by the commanding general and other senior officers; the lay-out of the approach to his big roomy office; the private 'crapper' he used, often guarded by an immaculate armed sentry when he was on the 'throne'; and the plan of the office as well. All that her contact needed now was the private ante-room, to which Patton withdrew to 'think things out' on occasion, in other words the place in which he took his afternoon nap when he had time. That piece of information she intended to obtain in the next day or so. For the furtive, one-armed French Army veteran and one-time German POW, who acted as her go-between, had already informed her it was vital that the 'chief', (whoever he was, she told herself) received the info as soon as possible.

Satisfied with what she had already achieved – indeed it gave her an almost sexual glow for some reason she couldn't quite define – she locked the plan away in her desk drawer once again and prepared her papers to meet the commanding general.

Just in time.

"Major," Jordan called, popping through the door with a perfunctory knock (a fact that annoyed her and immediately placed the unsuspecting clerk on her own personal 'shit list'). "The CG is about ready now. His aide, Colonel Codman, says for you to stand by with the info, ma'am." He stared at her flat homely face, a little puzzled by the sudden stern look on it. Had he done anything to offend her? he asked himself. Holy shit, he hoped he hadn't! Walker's corps was taking a beating on the Saar front and the corps commander was screaming for riflemen as replacements. They were even considering asking for Blacks to volunteer* Things had to be bad.

"It's a *Fubar*, Major," Patton exploded. "Not just a *Snafu* but a goddam down-to-earth *Fubar*.¶

Patton, his thin face flushed red, took her silence to mean he had offended the WAC major with his strong language and he added hastily, "If you'll forgive my French, Major."

She nodded, mentally taking notes of the position of the door to the ante-room and the easiest way to reach it from the office's big french window.

"If Ike had only given me the gas back in September instead of giving it all to that little Limey fart, Montgomery, I would have gone through Metz like shit through a goose." He clapped his hand, adorned with the West Point class ring, to his mouth and exclaimed, "There I go, cussing again, Major. You'll just have to forgive an old soldier, Major. I've been with rough-and-ready men too long. I've forgot my manners and

---

* At this time the US Army was strictly segregated. As a result there was only a handful of combat units made up of black US soldiers; and they were mainly commanded by white officers.
¶ *Fubar* – Fucked-up beyond all recognition. *Snafu* – Situation normal, all fucked up.

the courtesies in the presence of womenfolk." He gave a stiff little bow from his sitting position.

"Don't worry about it, sir, *please*," she answered. "I've heard worse from the enlisted men." She liked Patton. Often in the loneliness of her room at the HQ gazing at the picture of her dearly beloved long-lost Renate, she told herself that Patton was 'one of us. Pity his position prevents him from doing what he is naturally inclined to do.'

"Thank you, Major," Patton said with that thin wintry fake smile of his. "You indulge an old soldier in his whims."

"Yes sir," she said for want of something else to say, attempting to prolong her stay so that she could pick up as many details of Patton's office plan as she could.

"All right," Patton settled back in his big chair as he prepared for the boring routine of office work, though he would have much preferred being on the battlefield where the action was, "shoot the works. Tell me how much those Darkies and feather merchants back in the COMZ of yours are stealing from Third Army's gasoline allotments to sell on the Frog black market, the goddam crooks."

Dutifully she began to detail their nefarious activities telling herself as she did so that Patton was a general after her own heart; he was a person who could hate, especially Blacks and Jews . . .

Von Thoma held up his hand. Behind him the little convoy came to a halt, each man feeling for his weapon automatically. By now the L-Squad was a well-trained team. Its members didn't need orders to know what had to be done next. Von Thoma smiled tightly. His men were the best available in the *Wehrmacht* in this terrible winter of defeat in 1944.

Up front there was the first road block they had encountered since they had skirted Verdun and headed south to the Lorraine capital, Nancy. As von Thoma clambered stiffly from his jeep, he saw that it didn't look too formidable. Indeed it appeared to his trained eye to be very primitive: a couple of farm carts that could be wheeled away quickly, plus several bales of straw, all guarded by two bored GIs, with their rifles slung, and a fat gendarme, smoking although he was on duty and eating an apple at the same time. It was what they had called back in '39 when they had invaded Poland, 'a sixty-one-minute barrier' sixty minutes to erect and one minute to pull down again.

Lightly Schulze dropped from his own vehicle and joined him to survey the barricade, where the guards had still not noticed the appearance of the little convoy seemingly. "What d'yer think sir? One good puff and I could blow it down."

"Agreed," von Thoma said, eyes suddenly narrowing. "But look at that aerial to the right – in that wayside cottage at the rear. You know what that means. The *Amis* are in radio contact with someone or other. They might even have an operator inside the hut. A chap like that would be certain trouble, if you didn't nobble him before the balloon went up."

Schulze nodded. "*Einverstanden, HerrHauptmann,*" he growled and dropped his hand in the pocket of his camouflaged smock. When it reappeared, the knuckles of his right hand glistened dully in the faint winter sunshine. "The Hamburg Equalizer," he explained.

"The what?"

"Back in Hamburg on the waterfront, an undernourished sort of fellah like –"

Von Thoma opened his mouth to comment on that 'undernourished', but decided to say nothing.

"– me needed something to give him a bit o' muscle. So", he glanced down at the knuckle-duster, "I thought I'd get mesen a pair of brass knuckles. Now I think, sir, that I might deal with that operator quiet like . . ."

But Schulze would have no need of the famed 'Hamburg

127

Equalizer' of his that day, for just as von Thoma started to give him the order to go ahead, 'Doof the Sparks' came ambling across in his usual absent-minded manner, talking softly to himself as always, to say, "Change of plan."

Von Thoma looked at the dreamy-faced skinny radio operator with his big empty eyes. For his part Schulze touched his temple and whispered. "Nutty as a fruitcake, sir. Saw him giving the radio a big wet kiss not more than half an hour ago and last night—"

"Hold your water, Schulze," von Thoma interrupted the sergeant firmly. Everyone knew just how barmy all radio operators were. 'Doof', who looked exactly like the movie comedian* of the same name was no exception. Von Thoma ascribed their madness to the constant fiddling with their sets, straining to catch those distant messages in a dozen different European languages that they encountered daily. They simply lived in a dream world, remote from that of an ordinary mortal. "What's the matter, Doof?" he asked. "Where's the fire?"

"What fire, sir?" Doof asked in fresh bewilderment.

"Just an expression, Doof. What news do you have, man?"

"Change of plan, sir," the radio operator answered, shaking his head like a weary man trying to arouse himself from a deep sleep. "Orders from his nibs personally – I've forgotten his name. On the tip of my tongue—"

"Skorzeny, *Obersturmbannführer* Skorzeny?"

"That's the one, sir. Well, sir, we're to proceed to the Bismarck Rock immediately. The map reference is—"

"I know where the Bismarck Rock is," von Thoma interrupted him firmly. "Every German schoolboy does. We meet there then?"

"*Jawohl, Herr Hauptmann*," Doof tried to rescue the situation

---

* Dick und Doof, the German names for Laurel and Hardy, i.e. Fat and Stupid. Stupid Doof being Stan Laurel.

by being overly military, even clicking to attention, as if he were a raw recruit.

"All right, don't piss yersen," Schulze said coarsely. "The captain's got it." Doof looked enquiringly at von Thoma. The latter nodded. "All right, get back to your toys and inform HQ we'll be there. And don't kiss the frigging thing first."

"Kiss . . . kiss the thing," Doof stuttered as he staggered back the way he had come. "Nothing wrong with kissing . . . good night . . ." He shook his head, as if he simply couldn't comprehend the foolishness of his fellow men.

Quietly the two of them followed him, not taking their gaze off the barricade for a moment, but no one noticed their departure as no one had their arrival. Just before they reached the little convoy, von Thoma stopped Schulze and asked in a low voice, "You know what the Bismarck Stone is, don't you, Sergeant?"

"Course, sir. I'm not just a pretty face. Didn't the teachers stuff it down our throats every Sedan Day.* Why?"

"But do you know where it is?"

Schulze pushed his maroon beret forward and scratched the back of his shaven head.

THE SITUATION – LORRAINE, 2 DECEMBER 1944.

Von Thoma grinned in spite of his inner tension at the knowledge of what he was now going to have to order his men to do. At the same time though he thanked God for old hares like Sergeant Schulze and the rest. With soldiers like that behind he could go to hell and back, he was sure of it. They wouldn't let him down.

---

* 1st September, when Germany celebrated the victory over imperial France on that day at Sedan near the Franco-Belgian border.

"I'll tell you where it is." He cut short Sergeant Schulze's random wanderings. "It's on the heights above Metz to the west of the city. It's in *Ami* hands and probably just behind the front line."

Schulze whistled softly through his front teeth. "Christ on a crutch, sir. That means we're sticking our heads back in the pisspot."

"Not exactly. I've been thinking it over, Schulze. We're more likely to be stopped and grilled on the road to Nancy. After all, the *Amis* would probably want to know what a bunch of buck-toothed Englishmen are doing wandering around behind the line. Up front it's different. You know that."

"It's not much of a life for your ordinary common-or-garden stubble hopper," Schulze commenced in a well-rehearsed mournful tone, "up front. A jug o' suds, a bit of the old legover if he can find a piece of willing, steaming female gash and that's his lot—"

"Oh shut up, Schulze," von Thoma cut him short in sudden good humour, as he realised that the new order might be for the best after all. "You'll have me crying in my beer next. Back to our problem. What *Ami* footslogger is going to ask too many questions of a bunch of Englishmen moving up to the attack? After all, if the English are attacking and getting their damnfool turnips blown off, then it means *he* isn't. Get it?"

"Got it, sir," Schulze's broad tough face broke into a smile, too. "See what you mean."

"All right then, Schulze, get your thumb out and get the men turned round. We're heading for St Privat now – and I think this time there's gonna be little trouble from *Ami* roadblocks."

Five minutes later they were on their way following the straight French D road through the battle-scarred December landscape, heading for the pall of smoke which was Metz and the unknown . . .

Three

"Excuse my tit," Petra said in her demure little girl's voice and neatly tucked her huge dug back inside her low-cut blouse, as she rose from bending over *Standartenführer* Gross. She faced the impressed Rangers and added, "It makes me blush in front of all you men."

Hairless Harry scratched his crotch knowingly. "It don't exactly make me blush," he said after Savage, waiting anxiously for Gross to come to at last, had translated the huge whore's words.

Petra beamed. "I hope you don't think the worse of me. I'm only a helpless little woman really." She simpered at them and checked unconsciously if her breast was snugly tucked away inside her black leather bra.

Savage decided that his Rangers didn't need to know that she thought of herself as a 'helpless little woman', especially Pfc Peover, at whom Petra was now looking in a clearly predatory manner. So he didn't translate. Instead he said, "This guy knows something. We're sure of that. I want to get that info out of him – and quick!"

Hairless Harry clenched a fist like a small steam shovel and threatened, "Leave him to me, Major. I'll have him singing like a big yeller canary in five seconds flat."

"Not just yet, Hairless," Savage said hastily. He wanted the obviously terrified SS officer to sing, too, and in a hurry – for he knew time was running out; their cover wouldn't last for ever. All the same he didn't want any of the big bald-headed Ranger's strong arm methods – just yet.

At his lookout point, in the little watchtower used by the train's anti-aircraft lookouts on the top of the stinking coach, Peover whispered, "All clear, sir. A few looters about – and a Hun patrol. But they're keeping well clear of us. Now."

Savage nodded his understanding. During the night they had posted a chalk-written sign, standing at the head of the bombed goods train, stating, ACHTUNG – SEUCHEN GEFAHR . . . NIGHT ANNÄHERN!* Obviously it was working well. The Germans were well-known for their unreasoning fear of infectious diseases. He turned to the fat sweating SS man, his jowls already wobbling in anticipation of what he probably thought was the torture to come.

"*Jetzt*," he commenced slowly, stern yet not threatening, "what can you tell me?"

As if to emphasise that there could still be trouble if he didn't speak out, Petra cracked her whip.

This time the *Standartenführer* knew he wasn't facing some kind of relatively harmless sexual game, but a life-and-death situation. In his time he had seen many a poor wretch tremble and quaver in his presence when he had threatened to 'turn on the screws, if you don't give me what I want, you swine.' Now it was his turn and he was afraid. "I don't know. . . exactly," he quavered.

"What don't you know *exactly*?"

"What's going on . . . I'm not a military man, you understand . . . Really a humble office worker in uniform." He looked up hopefully at Savage and the latter told himself that those 'humble office workers in uniform' were the worst kind: merciless, without an ounce of pity running through that thin pink blood of their kind.

"But you know something," Savage urged. "You boasted as much as to Madame here, didn't you?" He indicated Petra, who

* Warning. Danger of Infection. Don't Approach.

132

towered above him, arms folded across that tremendous bosom straining to get out of the tight black silk of her blouse, as an envious Hairless Harry watched her, telling himself that he'd give his left nut – and then some – just to get his bald head between them tits and waggle it back and forth a couple of times. A guy could die happy after an experience like that!

"There is to be an offensive," Gross ventured.

"An offensive – where?"

"Here in the West. A few of us, who have dealings with the civilians and their affairs locally, have been informed and told to look out for any signs of treachery by the French. *Passeurs* . . . front-runners and the like."*

"Tell me more, Gross – *please*," Savage said, trying to contain his growing excitement. For three months the Western Allies had been trying to break the autumn-winter stalemate here on the frontier of the Reich, not expecting the Germans to take the offensive for one solitary moment. Now, it seemed, if *Standartenführer* Gross were right, that the Krauts were going to catch them with their drawers down about their ankles.

"Can you be more precise," Savage said and now there was iron in his voice. "Where is the *Wehrmacht* going to strike in the West. I want to know – and I want to know *now*." He clenched his fist significantly.

"That's the way to do it, Major," Petra encouraged him, as Savage stared hard at the SS officer's white shaken face, the eyes full of fear and apprehension now. "We want none of his piggery do we? Make the Boche talk, or by God!" Suddenly she slapped her whip against her booted right leg. Gross jumped as if he had been shot.

"To the north of here," he stuttered hurriedly.

"Do you know for certain?"

---

* Civilians who knew the frontiers intimately and could pass back and forth buying and selling information to the opposing forces.

"*Ja . . . jawohl, Herr Major,*" Gross cried, holding his pudgy hands in front of his face as if Savage might lash out at any moment. "I am certain. They will attack in Belgium after the special troops have killed your General Patton down here in Lorraine." The saliva was dribbling down from his slack mouth now in unreasoning fear and an ever-growing damp patch was spreading around his flies.

"*Du Drecksau!*" Petra exclaimed. "You dirty sow . . . you've gone and pissed yersen. Have you no frigging shame. I ought—"

"Say that again," Savage cut in rapidly. "About Patton. Quick, man . . . Let's have it."

The tears streaming down his terrified fat face now, Gross stared around at their hard faces, illuminated in the flickering yellow light of the candle, set in a saucer on a case in the centre of the straw-covered floor of the wagon. But if he were looking for pity there, he didn't find any. They were all too intent on getting the vital information from him.

"*Raus mit der Sprache!*" Savage hissed threateningly, mind racing wildly. "*Los, Mensch!*"

"Don't hit me . . . please . . . don't hit me," Gross quavered. "I'll tell you all I know. Before they attack in Belgium, they will kill your cowboy general – excuse – your *Herr General Patton*. They think that—"

The angry chatter of a machine gun drowned the rest of his words with startling suddenness. Up above in his lookout tower, Peover yelled, "*Krauts!*" Next moment he tumbled from his perch, hand clutching his right shoulder from which bright-red blood was spurting in a gleaming arc.

Hairless Harry was first off the mark. He always was when it came to action. He pushed the door of the flat car open with a heave of his mighty shoulders. It was still gloomy outside, but light enough to see. Up ahead on the twisted lines, the looters were lying full length, hands protectively over their heads. A few yards away a skinny-ribbed nag lay thrashing its hooves, fighting off death. But they were not the object of Hairless's angry gaze. It was those who had fired. He didn't have long to wait. Just at the corner of the shattered station with the old legend adorning its shell-pocked façade *'Räder Rollen fur den Sieg'* – wheels roll for victory – there was a sudden burst of vicious fire.

"Fucking Spandau," he yelled, "two o'clock and—" the rest of his words were drowned by the chatter of his tommy gun. A piteous scream and the enemy machine gun went suddenly silent. Slowly what looked like a red football, abandoned by some careless schoolkid, trundled off down the slope to the left. It was a severed head.

Savage watched it transfixed. But only for a moment. There was the sound of heavy nailed boots running. Whistles shrilled. Someone shouted an angry order. An air-raid siren started to wail mournfully. In an instant all was chaos and sudden violent death.

"Bug out . . . let's run for it," Savage yelled over the new burst of firing. " 'Kay, let's move, guys . . . AT THE DOUBLE!"

They needed no urging. They knew what would happen to them if they were caught, armed, behind the Kraut lines like this. They'd be shot out of hand. Someone grabbed the *Standartenführer*. He yelled in protest. Petra slapped him across his fat face. Silence. Peover, game as ever, despite his wound and useless arm, stumbled across to help her support the SS officer.

Then they were running and firing and stumbling down the littered track. Behind them the wild firing stabbed the grey gloom an angry scarlet. Once an old man in shabby field grey loomed up out of nowhere and raised a rifle. Savage shot him at five-yards range. He was lifted clean off his feet by the impact at such short range. He flew through the sir, as if propelled by an invisible fist and slammed into the side of a splintered bus.

A machine gun stopped any further flight abruptly. The tracer cut the air all around them in white lethal fury. Savage pulled out his last grenade. It hurtled through the air. *Crash. Boom!* In the blinding flash of sudden flame, they caught sight of the screaming crew flying in every direction. They ran on.

A German, half dressed, but with his bayonet fixed, came running out of a shed, with his braces flying. He was big, brutal and, with his bared teeth, intent on mayhem. Hairless Harry raised his tommy gun instinctively. Metal clashed on metal as Harry warded off the deadly thrust. But the man's weight made the bald-headed Ranger stagger. For a moment it seemed as if he would fall. The German thought so. He yelled, "Try this for size." He raised his bayonet once more for the lethal thrust.

Petra *die Peitsche* was quicker off the mark. "Arse with ears . . . don't you dare," she rumbled in that deep voice of hers. Her knee came up. It caught the German in the crotch. He dropped his rifle immediately. Frantically his hands flew to his injured parts, his false teeth bulging almost comically from his mouth with the sudden flood of vomit. Petra didn't give him a chance to recover. She kicked him again with all her strength. He fell without another sound, unconscious before he hit the ground.

Hairless Harry flung her a glance of intense gratitude. Despite their desperate situation, she blew him a wet kiss. "Eat yer frigging heart out, Pissover," he yelled exuberantly. *"She loves me!"*

He pelted on after the others, arms working like pistons, as slugs stitched a crazy pattern at his flying heels. For now the whole wrecked station had erupted into crazy, violent activity. Firing was coming from all sides. Here and there German soldiers were lobbing out stick grenades from the cover of their billets and, up on the signal tower, a sniper had taken up his perch and was beginning to attempt to pick off the running figures, zig-zagging from side to side in their attempts to put him off his aim.

Gasping and panting furiously like an ancient asthmatic in the throes of a final attack, Major Savage sought desperately for some way out of the trap. In mid-stride he paused and snapped off a shot at the German on the signal gantry. The slug howled off one of the signals and the sniper ducked momentarily. But Savage knew the breed. They were trained killers. He'd be up again in a moment, taking aim once more, trying to impress his CO with his lethal score. "*Shit on shingle*," Savage choked, as he ran on. "Give me wheels . . . wheels for Chrissake." But even as peered through the fog of war, stabbed seemingly everywhere by spurts of deadly flame, there seemed no answer to that prayer. He could not spot a vehicle anywhere. Behind him one of his Rangers flung up his arms with a little stifled cry of heartbreaking, utter despair. Next moment he slammed to the ground. The sniper was in business. He had shot his first victim.

Savage nearly gave up. But something, that old habit of command, concern for his guys, kept him going. "Keep running," he yelled frantically. "They'll fuckingly well shoot us if we surrender . . . KEEP GOING, GUYS!"

It was then that their luck changed. Afterwards, he could never explain it. How did that lone fighter-bomber from the RAF appear so startlingly and so suddenly out of the smoke of war over Mazières-les-Metz, so far away from the British sector of the front? And by the time he got around to attempting to find out, the surprise German *Unternehmen Bodenplatte** had killed their saviour and all the other pilots of his doomed squadron.

But there it was – a British Typhoon. It came zooming in at four hundred miles an hour. Its prop-wash swept all before it. The noise from its great Merlin engine was ear-splitting.

---

* The great last German surprise air attack of New Year's Day, 1945, which destroyed twenty-nine allied airfields in Europe.

Next moment it had opened fire with its cannon. The 20mm tracer shells streaked for the ground in a lethal white fury. Buildings splintered, fires started immediately, Germans fell on all sides. Up above the startled fugitives the signal gantry with its solitary sniper trembled and shook like a live thing. For what seemed an age, the spindly-legged metal structure appeared suspended in nothing, smoke pouring from its base where drums of oil had been set alight by the Typhoon's fire. Then with a great swish, the British plane came hurtling in yet again at breakneck speed. It flashed by the tower. That did it. Its prop-wash was too much for the spindly, dying structure. It came tumbling down in a shower of rending, tearing, splintered metal, bringing with it the sniper, his legs and arms moving frantically, a scream torn from his terrified lips, as he swam there in mid-air, vainly attempting to escape his certain fate.

The sniper slammed into the ground, his broken bones gleaming like polished ivory through the red gore of his split flesh. Next moment Savage sprang over his body and spotted the two trucks – great gas-driven monsters – both with gas-filled billowing rubber tanks in the trailers they towed. "Over . . . over here," he gasped with the last of his strength. Just behind him, Hairless Harry snapped off a burst at a driver who was pelting out from the air-raid shelter in an attempt to get into the first truck's cab. In vain. He went down as if his legs had been sawn off at the knee, while the British fighter, which had saved them unwittingly, soared into the sky beyond the grey gloom to disappear and meet its own fate.

Moments later the Rangers, those who had survived that perilous escape, were clambering aboard the truck and Hairless Hairy was swearing furiously, as he tried to start a reluctant engine. Another moment and they were on their way, leaving behind the dead and the dying, already stiffening rapidly in the December cold . . .

Four

M etz was dying.

And Savage and his Rangers were glad. Metz's death, they felt, might just save their own lives. That afternoon, as they had wound their way through the old town between the Cathedral and the *Porte des Allemands* near the river Meuse, the US dive bombers of the 9th TAC Air Force, working currently with Patton's army, had fallen out of the gloomy December sky in their scores.

They had flown in low from the west, dodging below the radar on the heights at Gravelotte, screaming in at roof-top height to carry out their deadly business even as the city's air-raid sirens had commenced shrieking the frantic warning. Above them as they zoomed back and forth, silver fish in the already billowing black smoke, flecked a cherry-red by the explosions below, cannon and machine guns chattering, the precise Vs of the Mitchell twin-engined bombers had appeared: squadron after squadron of them, advancing with grim purpose on their victim.

Then as the Lightnings and Mustangs had swept away, followed by the isolated bursts of machine-gun fire, they had started to release their deadly black eggs – hundreds of them. Nothing had been able to stop them. They had ploughed on through the black and brown network of anti-aircraft puffballs in invincible certainty, determined, it seemed, to wipe the ancient French city off the map.

And they had almost succeeded. As Hairless Harry had driven for cover in the skeletal trees on the other side of the little bridge at the *Porte des Allemands*, Petra had crossed herself like a little girl at her first communion and whispered a rapid prayer, while Harry had gasped, his broad face buffeted back and forth by the blast, "Jesus wept! They're clobbering the hell out of the place!"

Now the Mitchells went, their crews eager for their treat of eggs and ham and as much coffee as they could drink, leaving the sirens to sigh the 'all clear' and drag Metz's citizens, those who had survived, out of their cellars and air-raid shelters for the looting soon to commence.

Savage had seen it all before and, shocked as he still was by that tremendous pounding from the air, he knew they had to take advantage of the hysteria and mass confusion of the moment to clear the city while they could. He ordered Hairless Harry out from their cover and the truck lurched forward, great gas bag billowing out behind it, as they crawled through the burning façades of the eighteenth-century buildings, which trembled with each new slithering fall of masonry like theatre backdrops.

Looters were appearing – women, children and old men, with handkerchiefs tied across their mouths against the choking black smoke, carts on wheels tied to their waists, shopping bags in their hands ready to take away the loot, combing the wrecked buildings, ignoring the shattered gas lanterns jetting and gushing flame and the dead sprawled everywhere like ragged abandoned dolls. For the dead didn't matter. It was the living who counted – and the living needed food and drink to survive.

Now hardened as they were since they had first hit Omaha beach in June, the Rangers were shocked by what they saw on all sides: old women hacking at a dying horse with bread knives carving off huge chunks of bloody meat; a toddler suckling himself from a dead woman's swollen breast, her baby squawking in the gutter untended next to her; a woman, her skirt thrown up above her plump waist in total abandon, laughing, gasping, screaming with sexual joy as a German soldier pleasured her in full view on some rubble; an old man striking furiously at an equally old crone who had tried to take a bottle of wine from him; a crowd of women trampling over a man with two bloody stumps where his legs had been, crawling doggedly, as if he had just spotted the Holy Grail itself, to an open crate, full of bars of *Wehrmacht* chocolate.

"God . . . oh, God," Peover said incredulously, nursing his wounded limb, his young eyes full of horror, "how can people do such things . . . it's . . . the end of the world."

Savage caught the remark, but said nothing. It wasn't the end of the world by a long chalk, he told himself. There were no limits to the evil which human beings could perpetrate.

They battled on. More than once they drove down a side street – they were trying to avoid the main route out of the city towards American-held Verdun where they might be stopped – only to be turned back. For most of them were blocked by rubble and charred, blackened bodies. Once they had to fight off a mob of terrified German wounded in their blue-striped pyjamas trying to escape from a burning hospital, striking the sides of the truck with their crutches and sticks pleading to be taken with them. Savage risked a look backwards as they finally fended them off to see a blond-haired youth, totally naked save for his jackboots, crying, "*Kameraden . . . Hilfe . . . Ich kann nicht sehen . . . Help me God . . .* !" But the blond youth's pleas went unheard – on this terrible day, God was looking the other way.

They came to a crossroads. Savage knew where he was. He had memorised the map of Metz and area long before at the outset of their mission. To their right was the smoking, ruined Sepp Deitrich *Kaserne*. Back in '40 Hitler had celebrated

Christmas there with the victorious men of Sepp Deitrich's First SS. To the front was the D road which ran along the left bank of the Meuse heading south. To the right there was the main road which would wind up and around, rising to the heights which overshadowed Metz at Gravelotte where one of the great battles of the Franco-Prussian War had been fought back in 1870. The frontline was up there somewhere.

He hesitated, while the truck's engine ticked away noisily, the gas bag in the trailer sucking in and out like some great monstrous obscene lung. "Which way, Major?" Hairless Harry asked. "I don't want to hurry you, sir, but I think we're being followed." He jerked his head backwards. Savage peered into the side road. A platoon of German infantry, well strung out, was advancing cautiously down the littered gutter, rifles at the ready.

"Take your point, Hairless," he said. "The side road to the front. Nice and easy now. Don't want to arouse any suspicion."

"Roger, sir." Hairless said and let out the clutch. Gently and without too much smoke for a wood-gas powered vehicle, the *gazogene* moved off. Savage cast a look in the mirror. There was no reaction from the German patrol. Perhaps they were on the lookout for looters and deserters. They weren't interested in trucks.

"Keep it nice and slow, Hairless."

"Like a mother with a little 'un at her tit," he answered cheerfully.

Squashed up behind them Petra *die Peitsche*, who had obviously only understood one word of the order, felt for her massive breasts, as if to ensure that her dugs still remained in the security of the black leather bra. She gave a little, almost modest, sigh when she found they were.

At the wheel, Hairless said, "To get my head in between that pair and not know no pain for a half an hour and a guy could . . ."

The rest of his words were drowned by an urgent honking of a horn. Savage's heart skipped a beat. But he need not have feared. The driver of the motorbike, complete with side car, who had honked at them so noisily had swung by them daringly, skidding on two wheels round the crossroads, scattering a bunch of French refugees abandoning the stricken Lorraine city and was charging up the hill to Gravelotte the next instant, with the passenger in the side car, hooded and goggled, waving a cheerful goodbye to the startled, and not a little shocked, Rangers.

"Wow!" Hairless Harry breathed, as he followed Savage's order to slow down now that they were on the country road leading out of Metz. "I thought them Krauts on the motorbike had spotted us fer a minute."

"Yes, for a minute I thought the same. But they hadn't."

"Yeah." And then they forgot the Germans who had swept by them and concentrated on the dying groans of *Standartenführer* Gross, shot in the mêlée at Maziéres, who would never again 'suffer' under the lash of Petra *die Peitsche*, thus missing the encounter with the most celebrated German female spy of World War Two.

Not that the 'Grand Duchess', currently being driven up the circular heights that led to Gravelotte would have wished for that encounter on that grey December day so long ago now. Indeed she would never realise that their paths had ever crossed; for by the time she and Savage and his Rangers finally did meet, she would have less than an hour to live. She would die violently, a footnote in the secret history of World War Two, a mystery to the very end . . .

Five

S chulze shovelled down another great spoonful of dehy-
drated potatoes, sprinkled with looted US corned-beef
hash and a great dollop of something called 'ketchup', which
he had discovered in one of the abandoned *Ami* foxholes and
chortled to anyone prepared to listen, splattering mashed potato
everywhere as he did so, "Lovely fodder. Beats giddiup soup
and Old Man* any frigging day."

No one was prepared to comment. They, like the veteran
NCO, were too busy consuming the looted rations, smoking
in between bites, as if their very lives depended upon it.

All of them were squatting in the old trenches, crouched
low to dodge the bitter wind blowing straight from Siberia
across the barren, war-torn heights, glad at last to be able
to eat warm 'fodder' and be through the *Ami* lines safely,
though their own front line around Metz was still nearly a
kilometre away. In essence, they found themselves this grey
December afternoon with a hint of snow in the air, in a
kind of no-man's land. It was abandoned at the moment,
save for the unburied dead of both sides. But as soon as it
became dark, the old hares knew that the area would become
a hive of activity as friend and foe sent out patrols, started
mining, brought out the dead and commenced the hundred

* Horsemeat soup and canned meat, reputedly made from the bodies of
old men from Berlin's workhouses.

144

and one activities which were the infantryman's miserable lot at night time.

Von Thoma knew it, too. But he knew he had to stick it out in this dangerously exposed position between St Privat and Gravelotte at the Bismarck Stone until German Intelligence contacted him and gave him further orders. Besides his men of the L-Squad needed a rest, especially in view of what probably lay before them soon.

He crouched in the shelter of the weathered pear-shaped stone adorned by a fading Iron Cross and nibbled on his American ration biscuit and a piece of greasy, looted Spam. He could just make out the wording under the date 1870. It commemorated the illustrious *Schlachtenbummler**, who had stood here that summer and watched the Prussian Guard being decimated as it attempted to wrest the farm at St Privat from the French.

He screwed up his eyes and made out the names, Kaiser Wilhelm, General Phil Sheridan of the US Army (the US President's personal observer) and, of course, Bismarck, the 'Iron Chancellor' of Prussia, who had given this stone, set in the middle of a muddy French farmer's field, its name. He pursed his lips thoughtfully and finished his ration biscuit, pulling a face at the greasy taste of the Spam. Seventy-odd years before, the big shots had watched 20,000 Prussian Guardsmen charge that farm on the opposite side of the little road leading to Briey. Twice they had been hurled back with tremendous losses. The third time they had carried the day and the French defenders had retreated into the fortress of Metz below. A couple of weeks later the French had surrendered, and Prussia and her German allies had almost won the war. One year later, after Sedan, Bismarck had founded the Second Reich under Prussia.

* 'Battle fans'

Von Thoma's handsome young face, already scarred and marked indelibly by the years of combat since 1939, creased in a frown, one almost of bewilderment, as if he didn't quite understand the world. But to what purpose? Why had the bodies of those thousands of blue-uniformed Prussian Guards littered that same road in 1870? What had been achieved by it all? What would be achieved, indeed, by their own mission?

He stared at the Bismarck Stone, as if he might find the solution to his questions there. For it seemed to him on this cold December day in no-man's land that it was about time he began asking question – time, indeed, for all Germany's men and women to do that. Where had Bismarck, that gigantic East Prussian landowner, who had always worn uniform (complete with Iron Cross gained in that same 1870 war) though he hated the military, led the German people? Now where was his Austrian successor, Adolf Hitler leading them? To the destruction of Germany's Third Reich, just as Bismarck's Second one had been destroyed? He frowned. Lots of questions, but few answers. He wished he knew. He and 'old hares' like him were sick of just dying because they were ordered to do so for 'Folk, Fatherland and Führer'. They wanted some answers and they wanted them sooner rather than later before all of them were dead and could no longer pose the questions – "*Hauptmann . . . Hauptmann!*" Schulze's urgent hiss of warning cut into his reverie. He forgot Bismarck, Hitler and all the rest immediately. Once again he was one hundred per cent a front swine, living off his nerves, knowing that if he didn't react immediately and correctly, he and his men might well be dead before the hour was out.

He doubled forward to where Schulze was crouched, his mouth full of mashed potatoes. He flung himself into the trench, already unbuckling his holster, "*Wo brennst?*" he demanded urgently. "Where's it burning?"

"Over there, *Herr Hauptmann*, three o'clock . . . Next to the ruined barn. . . . Got it?"

"Got it."

While all around him his 'old hares' focused their weapons, the cold, the need for food and shelter forgotten now in an instant, von Thoma stared hard through the growing gloom at the French barn with the great yellowing tobacco leaves hanging and drying still from beneath the shattered eaves. Now he could hear it, too, the steady throb of a small engine and a rustling in the bushes which bordered the rutted, mud-filled farm track leading to the barn.

"Somebody's coming up the verge, chancing the mines,* parallel with the track, sir."

Von Thoma noticed a swaying in one of the bushes and nodded his agreement, but said nothing. He was too tense – too worried. His heart thundered in his ears and a vein was beginning to tick nervously at his left cheek. He realised that at long last, after nearly five years of combat, his nerve was beginning to go. "Hold on, Kuno," he told himself with a trace of bitter humour, "or the men in the white coats with the rubber hammers'll be leading you off to the funny farm."

Suddenly the engine stopped. It was followed by a loud echoing silence. The nerve at the side of von Thoma's face began to tick more furiously. Inwardly he cursed. Next to him Schulze raised his weapon, slowly, carefully. "Here they come, sir."

"Don't fire until I tell you, Schulze."

Schulze nodded, but said nothing. His gaze was fixed exclusively on the bushes at the side of the farm track.

Von Thoma caught the blur of a face. He slipped off his

* Anti-personnel mines would usually be sown at the sides of the tracks to catch the unsuspecting soldiers dismounting from their vehicles.

safety. In a moment the bloody business of killing would commence. Christ, would there be no end to it?

But that wasn't to be – this time. "*Friedrich*," a voice hissed. It was a soft, almost feminine sound.

"The password, sir."

It was. Von Thoma's heart leapt with joy. *Friedrich* was the first part of the name of the place where Bismarck was buried. Hurriedly he completed the name, hardly recognising his voice as he did so, "*Ruh*".

Next moment a tall slim figure, dressed in military uniform without badges of rank or decoration rose from the bushes, busy putting back a Walther pistol in its holster. "What a fucking carry-on," that oddly female voice said and next moment their contact was running lightly towards them and the hip movement left no doubt now that this indeed was a woman.

Minutes later she was seated in their midst, what looked like a flying helmet, complete with goggles thrust to the back of her short cropped hair, puffing away gratefully at one of their American cigarettes, gushing, "I say my hair must look a frightful mess, but these *Ami* cigarettes are really something. Why they make me almost want to spill my cookies – they're so strong. But what a treat after that horseshit that we usually have to smoke . . ." And on she babbled gaily, as if the front line were a million kilometres away and they listened, mouths gaping like village yokels. They had met the 'Grand Duchess'.

They were fascinated, although, as she babbled away, seemingly totally unaware of the circumstances in which she found herself, she wasn't the type of woman their kind associated with. In the last few years, their choice of woman had been limited to whores, war widows out to 'forget everything' or simple country girls, impatient to be raped, happy to have been allowed to lose their virginity in a hayloft. They lived short, brutish lives; they had no time for any other kind of woman or 'gash', as they called them crudely.

The Grand Duchess, and the handful of them who would survive would always think of her under that title, was sexually abandoned, that was for sure; her speech was well larded with the rough terms they used themselves. But she obviously lived, for all that, on a completely different plane from them. Even the minor aristocrat *Hauptmann* von Thoma soon realised that.

"Of course," she said, "once they realised that I had no taste for the male organ—" she laughed and puffed hard at her cigarette, wrinkling her eyes against the smoke. "Oh God, what am I saying? Taste for the male organ indeed . . . Well, they used me in that sphere. Our beloved Führer might well be a sexual eunuch, at least the dummies who make up the German 'Folk'," she emphasized the term contemptuously, "think he is. But there are those in the Party whose tastes are a little more sophisticated . . . more specialised, if you know what I mean, *Herr Hauptmann.*?" She gave von Thoma what he supposed was a vampish, come-hither look and he actually blushed. "My chief – Father Christmas – he could see the potential in my unfortunate – er affliction immediately." Again she giggled and for the first time since he had met her under these very strange circumstances von Thoma realised that beneath her supposed frivolity there was a very serious person indeed. "How?" he asked.

"To go after influential people – women to be exact. You must realise that there are some very important women out there, women whose tastes are quite liberal, even though they might be the wives or mistresses of important men. You know the English prince and his American woman . . . the French prime minister and his mistress . . . that Rumanian king . . ." She laughed at the look on von Thoma's handsome face and instinctively reached and patted him, as if she felt she might have offended him by her revelations. "Don't take it so

149

bierernst,* Hauptmann. There are many sophisticated people who have sophisticated tastes, as I have just said, including both men and women."

"Yes, yes," he agreed hastily, deciding that the conversation with this Grand Duchess was going nowhere. "But if I may interrupt?"

"You may." She lit another cigarette from her last one, her fingernails red, as if they had been painted with blood.

"Well – er . . . Grand Duchess—"

She chuckled, but didn't comment on his hesitant, embarrassed use of the title.

"What you have to say is—" He changed tack. "We were told that we had to report here for further briefing. Now I don't see what you have said has got to do with our mission. If you'll forgive me saying so."

"Of course, I'll forgive." She stubbed out her cigarette and leaned forward impetuously, so that he could scent her peculiar fragrance of tobacco smoke and perfume. "But all will be revealed in due course. You see," her eyes twinkled mischievously, "I'm going with you . . . You'll need me. In a way, I'm going to be the key in the door." And with that she started to laugh, as if she would never cease, while they stared at her, unshaven, open-mouthed, in complete bewilderment . . .

---

* Admiral Canaris, head of the German Secret Service, known thus on account of his show of white hair and benign appearance: 'beer serious'.

Six

The enemy caught them completely by surprise.

Naturally Savage knew that they were in constant danger being in the general area of the front line, but he'd chanced it, telling himself that the Germans would concentrate most of their resources around the endangered forts to the west of Metz. For it was there that General Patton was attacking. But he had guessed wrong.

He had ordered his men to dismount five kilometres from Metz, not too far from the Meuse and check out what appeared to be a typical abandoned hamlet of the area: a dozen or so tumbledown eighteenth-century houses grouped around a cobbled square, complete with the usual rusty iron bandstand, a bold *Poilu* statue commemorating the First World War and dominated by an onion-domed church.

Obediently his men had slunk into the shadows on both sides of the one village street. Like timber wolves on the prowl they pushed into the *place*, weapons at the ready, but yet relaxed. For there was no sign of life about the village, not even the angry barking of an abandoned dog or the lowing of a milk-heavy heifer in the stalls. Indeed most of their minds were on the cheering prospect of being under cover, with a possibility of some fresh meat taken from an abandoned animal, if they could find one in this deserted village.

Up in the lead, Hairless Harry had just placed his out-stretched fingers on the top of his helmet the infantry sign for 'rally on me', when the moon had slid from the ragged clouds and illuminated the square to their front in its cold icy light. It was then that all hell had been let loose. They had not even comprehended the harsh guttural order – "*Halt . . . stehenbleiben . . . oder ich schiesse,*" when a Schmeisser had opened up at close range. Like a flight of angry hornets, a salvo had cut the air just above a startled Hairless Harry's head, bringing down a shower of masonry chippings on the Americans. Then the fight had commenced. For Savage realised immediately that there were German infiltrators to their rear, where they had left the *gazogene* truck. He could hear their shouts, queries, calls to one another. As Hairless Harry gasped at his side, "Gee, sir, they really have got us by the dong this time."

And Savage knew he was right. The Germans really had.

Another angry burst ripped across the cobbles of the *pavé*. Blue sparks ripped towards them. Savage yelped as a stone fragment struck. Blood started to pour down the side of his face. Next to him, Hairless Harry, hit too, but also not seriously cried, "Fuck this for a game o' soldiers!"

Savage made a decision, as angry flashes of violet light stabbed the darkness from the direction of the baroque church. He knew, even as he bellowed the order, that he might well be making a fatal mistake. But what alternative did he have? They'd be slaughtered where they stood if they remained out in the open much longer. "Into that house – the big one – over there. At the double there," he yelled above the noise of the firing.

The men needed no urging. The door was locked. It didn't stop the Rangers. While the others covered them, two of the sweating cursing soldiers shot away the great rusty ancient lock and then battered the door open with their butts. An NCO ran towards them, "For you, ze war is over," he yelled triumphantly in stage English. "Hands up!" Hairless Harry let him have a burst in the guts. Another German leaned out of a window. In the lurid light of the fire fight, a Ranger spotted the stick grenade in his hand. The Ranger acted first. The man cried out with the pain as the slug from the Ranger's M1 slammed into him. The shock seemingly confused the German. He didn't let go of the grenade. It was a fatal mistake. Next moment it exploded in an angry yellow burst of flame and grey smoke. His hands were almost severed. When the smoke cleared, they could see him hanging there, unconscious, what appeared to be two blood-red mittens dangling from his white wrists. A moment later they were bundling into the dark smelly hall of the old house, which stank of garlic, ancient lecheries and human misery, and were safe – for the moment.

Before she had taken up her new exotic role as Petra *die Pietsche*, she had played a more humble one as Paula Schmitt, pavement pounder and, in the year 1941, 'Volunteer Comforts for the Troops, North Sector,' servicing the 116th 'Greyhound' Panzer division in South Russia – "more like frigging bulldogs than greyhounds", she had often moaned about the conduct of her 'clients'.

But before she had left for Berlin to take up 'advanced training in the service of senior officers' and had been transformed into that *grande horizontale*, Petra *die Poitsche* had learned a great deal about military matters. It had been highly necessary in the broad spaces of Russia where surprises, military and otherwise, seemed to occur every day. As she had always warned new recruits to the Greyhounds Mobile Brothel Number Sixty-Nine. "It's a wise girl who knows when to lift up her knickers – if she happens to have them on, that is – and run for it. Otherwise she's gonna have a regiment of smelly Ivans sticking their dirty communist things into it."

Now as the gunfire erupted so suddenly to their front in the supposedly abandoned Lorraine hamlet, she didn't collapse into tears and 'have me monthlies', as she would have put it, if asked, in her own inimitable style. Instead she reasoned what to do next, basing her judgements on eighteen months" service at the front, during which she had won the 'War Service Cross, First Class with Swords' plus the 'Frozen Flesh Order, Number Two'* ("And I ain't telling yer, nosey, what part of my alabaster body got frostbite either, so there!").

Should she run? But if she did, she would have to abandon the Rangers' wounded inside the *gazogene* truck, including the handsome young Pfc Peover, whom she fancied rotten. Or should she hide until the trouble was over, keeping her eyes on her wounded charges?

In the end, as the noise of the approaching German patrol came ever closer, she decided to do neither. "What yer got them milk factories up front for?" she asked herself boldly. "And yer've got a pair of legs that could squeeze the life outa a client better than any poxy python – and with more fun as well."

In a minute she had worked out a rough-and-ready plan. She nodded to Peover lying on the floor of the truck peering out into the glowing gloom a little helplessly. Very deliberately, hoping he would understand, she made the gesture of someone pulling the trigger of a pistol with his thumb and forefinger. Peover looked back at her puzzled. But she could not spend any more time explaining now. She had her task to carry out – and quick – for they were almost upon her. In a matter of moments they would spot the truck and its wounded. Hastily she grabbed the front of her blouse and pulled with all her strength . . .

Hairless Harry ripped off a burst from his M1. A German running across the road skidded to a sudden stop, his knees buckling beneath him like those of a new-born foal. "Hot shit," Harry exclaimed in delight. "Plugged the bastard."

---

* The soldiers' nickname for the frostbite order awarded to those soldiers who had suffered that complaint during the fighting in Russia.

"Watch your ammo," Savage warned dourly. "We're running out."

Yet another grenade sailed through the burning night and exploded against the wall of the house. A window splintered. Glass flew everywhere. Hot air flew in. "Get that window!" Savage cried desperately. "They'll use it – the bastards!"

Just in time. Hairless leaned out, ready to pull in the shutter, splintered as it was, when another burst ripped the length of the wall. He sprang back. Not for long. His face powdered grey with stone dust, he pressed his trigger. There was a curse, a shrill scream, a bellowed order and then everything went silent from that particular area.

Savage shouted out his encouragement, then fire submerged the building once again in full fury and like the rest of the handful of desperate defenders he was fully occupied trying to keep them at bay with Hairless Harry whooping, "And another pesky Redskin bites the dust!" No one laughed . . .

No one did some seventy metres to the rear as the German attackers skidded to a halt at the amazing sight of that massive woman, naked to the waist, all her opulent charms outlined in the lurid flickering light of the roof blazing away opposite.

"Great crap on the Christmas Tree!" one of them exclaimed; he instinctively lowered his weapon as Petra lifted up one of her huge breasts and waved it to him as if in welcome. Another of them gasped, "Get in between them tits, comrades, and yer'd never come out alive agen."

"*Genug!*" their platoon commander cried as his men stood there in the open, making perfect targets against the background of the burning building. "Ain't yer seen a gash's milk factory afore?"

In the back of the truck Peover ignored the pain of his wound. Next to him another Ranger who had been shot in the leg, raised his rifle as well, and both of them took aim on the stupified Germans standing in the open, almost within reaching distance.

"Why don't you, gentlemen, come on over," Petra cried, rotating the breast she was holding playfully. "If you stand in line, I'll take care of you all. Never fear," she added, praying that the men hidden in the back of the truck were ready – she couldn't keep up this deadly charade much longer, "you'll all get a turn at what Mummie's got to offer." She pulled up the huge dug with its painted nipple and touched the scarlet tip with her tongue like some doting mother might, planting a gentle kiss on the naked rump of her adored baby.

"Holy strawsack," one of the soldiers hissed broken-voiced, grabbing at his bulging crotch. "Five minutes of that and I could frigging well die a happy man—"

Crack! The soldier who had spoken would never get his five minutes of happiness; he started and looked down instinctively at his no longer bulging crotch, as if the source of the trouble might be down there for some unknown reason. It wasn't. Slowly a dark red circle began to widen on the front of his tunic. Next instant he fell face forward, dead before he hit the battle-littered cobbles.

In that very same instant, Petra threw herself down with surprising speed for such a huge woman. Just in time. In the back of the truck, the other Ranger opened up with his semi-automatic Garand rifle. Germans went down on all sides, caught completely off guard. In a flash the *pavé* was littered with dead and dying bodies.

The platoon leader, shot in the leg, but still on his feet, hopped around, as if looking for cover yelling frantically. "Return the fire, you frigging cardboard soldiers. The bastards are in the back of the truck. Return—" His enraged command ended abruptly in a shocked gasp as the bullet from Peover's rifle caught him squarely in the face. Suddenly it looked as if someone had thrown a handful of strawberry jam at his features. He reeled back, his face dripping onto his chest. A moment later he lay threshing wildly in his death agonies on the *pavé* and Petra, on her feet, once more, was shouting. "Come on. *Los Manne* . . . we must help the others!"

Peover, quicker on the uptake than the other Ranger, clambered painfully over the truck's tailboard, feeling his wound begin to bleed once more, but ignoring it. Instinctively he knew what to do. Swaying a little, trying to maintain his balance, he cried in a voice he hardly recognised as his own, "All right, A Company . . . at the double. You men of B Company stand by to—" He swayed, almost as if he might faint, and grabbed the tailboard with his free hand.

"Brav Jung," Petra called in admiration. She would dearly liked to have rushed to his aid, but she knew there was no time for that. Instead she kept up the shouting in French, as if a whole regiment were attacking the Germans up the street around the church. Meanwhile the Ranger, who was unable to stand, had begun to fix long grenades to the end of his rifle and was firing them like a mini-mortar at the unseen enemy, also shouting at the top of his voice between each firing.

Five minutes later it was all over. The Germans attacking Savage and the main body panicked. Petra's trick had worked. They thought they were being attacked by a company-strength *Ami* unit to the rear, one of the many which had been infiltrating their lines for weeks now from Patton's Third Army. They fled, not even attempting to collect their wounded.

Minutes afterwards, when Peover managed to drive the truck to where Savage waited, bleeding heavily again as he was, the trapped men gawped at the still half-naked Petra. She savoured her triumph, finally attempting to stuff away those tremendous breasts, until Hairless Harry broke the astonished silence with an apt, "Titty takes all, I guess."

A dozen miles away, the L-Squad had decided, just as Savage had, that the time was ripe to head west. It appeared the front was unsettled, but confused; and again it was a woman, who got the ball rolling. The Grand Duchess came back from behind the bushes, where, as she had put it moments before in the language of the 'front swine', "Got to take a piss. My tonsils are floating," saying, *"Los, Herrschaften.* Don't stand around like a spare dildo in a convent. *Let's move it!"*

They moved it. Minutes later they had disappeared into the silver darkness heading for their date with destiny. Two groups of disparate soldiers, led and encouraged by two of the strangest women to emerge from that unknown war in the shadows, on their way to the final showdown, which might well seal the fate of Europe for the rest of the twentieth century . . .

PART IV

I don't expect to be sixty years old. Not that that is old,
but I simply prefer to wear out from hard work before then . . .
or better to be killed by the last bullet of the last battle.

General Patton, Dec 1944

PART II

One

"Ike here – Georgie?"

Patton took the forbidden cigar out of his mouth and spoke urgently into the red telephone. Outside in Nancy it was snowing. People were hurrying by, shoulders hunched against the heavy wet flakes. One of his MPs had dodged into a doorway and was having an illegal smoke while on duty. Patton didn't blame him; he would have done the same if he had been outside in this bitter December weather. The locals were already maintaining it was going to be the coldest winter for a quarter of a century. "Ike," he answered. "Business or pleasure?"

"Business."

Patton sat up. "Okay General, I'll scramble now."

"Do, Georgie," Eisenhower, the Allied Supreme Commander, far away in Paris answered.

There was a series of clicks, followed by pauses, and the line between Versailles and Nancy was ready for use. "Shoot, General," Patton snapped.

"'Kay, Georgie." As Patton's superior Eisenhower could still use Patton's nickname. "The Jerries have bitten," he exclaimed, his delight clear even over a hundred and fifty miles or so.

"Hot dog! You don't say, General."

"I do, Georgie," Eisenhower answered in high good humour. "Our listening patrols out in the Eifel across the German border from the Ardennes have reported much increased activity there.

161

The locals have got the breeze-up and are moving so they know that the balloon's soon to go up. Most importantly, the Krauts have gone on radio silence since twenty-four hundred hours last night all along the front in the Ardennes – and you know what that means, Georgie?"

Patton certainly did. Armies always went on radio silence, in order not to give positions away, when they were about to go over to the offensive. "Any idea when exactly?"

"Roughly," Ike answered a little more thoughtfully. "We're expecting a low from the north – Arctic Circle way – and you know what that means? Poor flying weather and when there's poor flying weather we lose the great advantage of the air superiority we have over the Krauts. So when do they go over to the offensive? I don't need to tell you, do I Georgie?"

"Certainly not, sir. As soon as our ships can't fly."

"Exactly."

Patton paused. He wasn't a sensitive man in any way. He was wont to quote the old French saying to excuse casualties in battle – you can't make an omelette without cracking eggs. All the same, he thought at that moment, just how cynical Eisenhower was. It was not just a calculated risk that Ike was running on the Ardennes front by thinning out the troops and chancing that the Krauts wouldn't attack there. It was a deliberate strategy. He *wanted* the Germans to assault his four weak divisions there with as much strength as they had. In that way Ike would draw them out of the bloody fortification of the Siegfried Line and finally allow his armies to commence mobile warfare in Germany itself. But how many mothers" sons were going to die in the process? That was something that didn't seem to concern the Supreme Commander one goddam bit. Patton shrugged and dismissed the matter. He knew the role he was going to play in the great scam and he was intent on making the most of it. After all, the thing that mattered was that Patton and his Third Army grabbed the headlines back home as the force that finally stopped the Krauts.

"So it's on, General?" he said.

"It is, Georgie," Eisenhower said firmly.

"When, sir?"

"Intelligence says that we can expect the Continent to get socked in by Saturday December 16th, Georgie. Naturally we're not getting anything from the backroom boys at Bletchley.* But the bad weather to come and the fact that Air Recon had spotted no more, other than the normal trains, crossing the Rhine heading for the Eifel seem to indicate that it's gonna be – with perhaps eighty per cent certainty – that Saturday." He paused and added with a chuckle in his voice, "Happy Christmas for the Jerries, eh?"

"Yessir," Patton was in no mood for humour. His mind was racing with the things he would have to do before that fatal Saturday. "Thanks for the tip, General. I've taken my best two infantry divisions out of the line ready for the move north into the Krauts' left flank and my Fourth Armored is already on standby for the same task."

"Supplies – and above all, gas, Georgie?"

"All taken care of. But I'm asking for an extra one hundred thousand gallons of gas from those feather merchants at COMZ to be on the safe side, General."

"You'll get them, Georgie. Don't worry about that. I'll talk to those – er – feather merchants – here in Paris personally. So, Georgie, that's about it. All we've got to do now, is to sit and wait for the Krauts to make their move."

"Agreed, sir. But will the guys of Middleton's Corps –" he meant the four divisions of American troops in the Ardennes

---

* The greatest British decoding operation at Bletchley Park in the English Home Counties.

"– be alerted when the shit hits—" he corrected himself hastily "– the balloon goes up, sir?"

Eisenhower hesitated, then he said straight out. "No, George. We can't have the Krauts being warned by a prisoner at the very last moment. We want the Krauts out of their goddam Siegfried Line out in the open where we can kill them easily and get the Army moving. We've pussyfooted around too long as it is – ever since last September. No, George, the guys of Middleton's Corps will have to take their chance just like the rest of us. Best of luck, George." The phone went dead.

Patton looked at it with a cynical grin before he replaced it on its cradle, turning off the scramble switch. "Take their chance like the rest of us," he mused half aloud, and wondered what kind of lethal chance the Supreme Commander was taking in that eighteenth-century cathouse of his in Versailles, surrounded by his fawning cronies, their mistresses and their goddam lap dogs. His smile broadened. Chance of not getting his pecker up when that red-haired, green-eyed limey mistress of his asked him to perform in the hay. He dismissed the problem and hit the button of his 'squawk box'. "Charley," he called in high good humour suddenly.

Codman, always there when wanted, replied promptly, as if he had been waiting at his own desk in the outer office all the time just for this summons. "Sir?"

"Things are rolling, Charley. Can you get me that GI with the built-in foxhole," he said crudely. "Not that anyone would want to use that dame's foxhole – not with that goddam moustache of hers."

"You mean the WAC Major, sir – er, Major Hartmann of POL?"

"That's the one."

"Sir?"

"I need the dame here PDQ."

"Pretty damned quick it is, sir."

Half an hour later Major Hartmann emerged from Patton's office in a flustered hurry. Patton hadn't been his usual charmer with the ladies this particular morning. He had been instead the impatient army commander in a hurry, who brooked no delay and no excuses. She had managed to reassure him – with some difficulty, it had to be admitted – that the last major shipments of oil fuels would reach the Third Army railhead at Nancy within the next forty-eight hours. "You'd better be right, Major," had been his parting words, narrow lips taut, face threatening, "or heads will roll otherwise."

She had pretended to be impressed by the threat, but as she had left, she had told herself, that if anybody's head was going to roll in the next forty-eight hours, it would be General Patton's cropped greying one. Now while Pfc Jordan rang number after number on the outer phone, making sure that her promise to the Army Commander would be fulfilled on time, Major Hartmann sat in her own cubbyhole musing. In these latter years ever since she had been told to join the WACs by 'them', she had not experienced much pleasure of a personal nature. There had been a sergeant, a great hulk of a woman with a trace of some Eastern European accent, back in training in '42. She had treated her like a little girl, but she had been heavy-handed and had smelled horribly of garlic and an unwashed body.

In England in '43, she had been taken up by a group of well-born women, some of whom had aristocratic titles and wore horsey suits to go with their horsey 'county' looks. For a while it had been great fun, but they had dropped her once she had been posted to Patton's Third Army in Cheshire. Again she had realised that professional lesbians were really only interested in sex control and power; they had no time really for love. Here in Nancy and Paris she had taken up with much younger French women who were pathetically grateful for the goodies with which she could shower them

– black-market cigarettes, nylons, chocolate and the like. Here she was in control. But again she knew that – sadly – it wasn't really love. Indeed she suspected that behind her back, while swearing undying devotion, they were sleeping with GIs or anything else in trousers.

Captain Hartmann sighed. How different *she* had been in what she now thought of as her days of wine and roses. She was sure that *she* had really loved her for herself; and besides *she* had been the one who had seduced her and made her aware of her real inclinations and needs. *She* had been her first great love. Again the gross woman with a trace of a moustache sighed like a love-sick schoolgirl, totally unaware of Jordan outside crying almost desperately, "But the Major says you promised that shipment for today, Sarge. Christ Almighty, this could cost me my job!" For once again she was in Washington in that glorious wonderful, unforgettable summer of 1940.

How she had ever met the Grand Duchess, as everyone had called her, she never recalled afterwards. Perhaps she had not wanted to. Perhaps she did not want to believe that blonde lithesome European, with the shaggy cropped hair, something like Ingrid Bergman in *For Whom the Bell Tolls* of that same 1940, had experienced another life before they had met. Nor – at first – had she been able to explain how the Grand Duchess had wanted to take up with her, a plain lowly stenographer from the rural Mid-West who had a low paid Civil Service job at the White House. Why, the foreign girl, who had seemed to her completely uninhibited, saying what she liked, doing what she liked with apparently not a moment's thought that she might well be stepping on the toes of someone important in status-conscious Washington, had sought her out was beyond her – *then*. After all she had the entrée to Washington's Nob Hill society, and, most importantly, to no less a person than the President's wife herself.

Why Eleanor Roosevelt with her homely looks and protruding

teeth, her life centred on good causes, had ever taken up with the Grand Duchess, she had never been able to comprehend – at first. Here was the Grand Duchess, a German, an aristocrat and from her speech an anti-Semite, accepted by a very liberal Mrs Roosevelt, whose husband hated Germans, especially those of the Junkers class, and who, herself, even invited and *entertained* coloureds in the White House! Later, after she and the Grand Duchess had slept together that Christmas with the snow falling softly outside the ski lodge and a view stretching to the snow-capped mountains fifty miles away, as if they were the only two people left alive in the world, she had found out. But by then there had been no backing out of the web of intrigue that the Grand Duchess always spun around herself wherever she went, not that she had wanted to. She had been even prepared to betray her country for the love of the beautiful German seductress. Not that that had worried her greatly either. America was the land of male pigs, who thought solely of that itch in their loins. They knew nothing of a woman's special longings and desires. So why should she feel ashamed at betraying them and the country which they ran solely for their own sex?

Suddenly, quite startlingly, she felt a surge of sexual desire at the thought of that Christmas so long ago. It had been all so innocent – totally unlike the contrive paid couplings of her present life – so natural, so loving. If only she could re-create that time! Perhaps now that the Grand Duchess had made a reappearance so abruptly, there might be a chance . . . Oh, God if only there were! She felt her heart began to thump almost painfully and her gross homely face was contorted with something akin to longing so that Jordan outside would never have recognised her as the soulless, super efficient superior, who he would never have suspected of having a single human weakness. Indeed he might have remarked, when questioned: "Major Hartmann *human*? Hell no. That dame's got a calculating machine for a heart and stenographer's ink for blood."

"Major!"

For a moment, entranced still with the vision from that dreamlike Christmas, of a naked Grand Duchess folding her into her arms and whispering into her ear, the cunning fingers of her right hand already deep inside her, "Darling, I'm going to make you happier than you have ever been before in your whole life", she could not comprehend where she was until Pfc Jordan called once again, "Major!"

"Yes, Jordan," she answered, shaking herself like a person finding it hard to wake from a deep sleep.

"It's Base Supply, Major," he called through the open door. "They've got a problem."

The dream vanished. She grasped the phone on her desk with her heavy hand, the fingers stained brown with nicotine, growling almost angrily. "Not yet they haven't, Jordan . . . But they soon goddam will."

In the mirror opposite Jordan shook his head at his own image and momentarily folded his hands as if saying a prayer. "Brother," he whispered. "Now the shit really does hit the fan . . ."

Two

"*Kamaraden*", she announced in the easy-going manner of hers that entranced von Thoma's hairy old hares, "the road from Salines to the *Ami* airfield at St Max." With the bayonet she had borrowed from Sergeant Schulze, transformed from the rough-and-ready NCO, whose motto was 'Gash and Suds, that's all that matters for yer average front swine,' to a gallant, all bowing and scraping and calling the Grand Duchess 'your gracious miss,' she drew a line in the frozen dust, cutting through the layer of snow. "Twenty-odd kilometres away, soon in for a surprise visit from our famed 'Hunters from the Sky'"*

"Paras?" von Thoma asked sharply.

She flashed him that wonderful white smile of hers, pure beauty and truth seeming to radiate from her open face. "*Genau.* It's a new dimension, courtesy Herr Skorzeny. A small group are to land at St Max."

"A diversion?"

"Yes," she said. "Naturally it will alarm Patton's HQ, but we hope it will draw off his guard company."

"I see," von Thoma said with a wry smile. The *Abwehr* agent from Admiral Canaris' secret service, seemed to be taking over the op. But it didn't worry or annoy him. She was an exceedingly competent person. "But won't it alarm all other *Ami* units in the area, as well?"

*Fallschirmjager. Literally, hunters from the sky (or by parachute).

169

"Naturally. But I think that should be to our advantage too. In the confusion there will be less of a chance that anyone might stop us" – von Thoma noted that 'us', but didn't stop her at that moment – "and ask what a group of English soldiers is doing here deep behind US lines." She paused as if she half expected questions, but when none came, she continued in that so very reasonable, totally confident manner of hers, as if she went on life-or-death missions every day before breakfast. "As the panic starts, we move at all possible speed through the centre of Nancy from the east, using the *Place Stanislas* route – the enemy surely wouldn't expect a bunch of German killers risking that route – and head for Patton's HQ at *Rue Auxerre*."

Von Thoma thought it was time to comment. He took his eyes off the grey wintry sky, a habit which he had acquired ever since he had been transferred to the western front and he had learned always to keep an eye out for enemy aircraft which dominated the sky, and said, "But if you have created mass confusion *outside* Nancy with this paradrop, won't you have caused the same mess in Patton's HQ? People will be running around like headless chickens and that should make it damnably difficult for us to find the General." He refrained from saying, 'and kill him'.

"No," she answered without the slightest hesitation. "There's been another alteration to the plan *Hauptmann von Thoma*."

Schulze looked at his officer significantly, though he, too, was obviously bowled over by the Grand Duchess and the manner in which she seemed to have taken charge. As he would remark to his cronies afterwards, "I've never seen a piece o' gash like that since Big Bertha, caught on her own and having to service a company of the 50th, lined 'em up into two groups. Needy and Very Needy. Some organiser that woman. Naturally I was in the group of Very Needy," he added boastfully. "If I don't get it twice a day, comrades, I think I'm going impotent."

Von Thoma ignored the look. The woman knew what she was about. Besides he was too eager to learn what else she had up her sleeve to comment on anything, so he waited for her disclosure.

Next moment she let them have it. "We have a little friend inside General Patton's HQ. In fact she's been there for a long time. This friend is the one who has supplied us with a right-up-to-date plan of the HQ's layout. Now as soon as they are alerted in Nancy that there has been a paradrop at Max, our friend will sabotage the blackout system in the area of General Patton's quarters."

"How do you mean?" von Thoma asked quickly.

She looked up at him and smiled, obviously pleased with what she saw. He, for his part, thought that the Grand Duchess would be worth a sin or two, but he guessed that would never come to pass. "It's quite simple. She'll ensure that the blackout curtains – shutters – or whatever the *Amis* use are opened so we'll have a lighted arrow, as it were, leading us straight to the General's quarters. She is one hundred per cent certain that she can—"

"*She?*" he queried sharply in the same instant that the air sentry cried, "Plane approaching low from the north. Attention – plane approaching."

All eyes were raised in the direction indicated. Coming in very low, barely skimming the tops of the skeletal winter trees, was a light plane, the kind the Americans used for artillery target observation. It was clear that it had spotted the L-Squad, as they squatted at the side of the lonely D road. It was definitely coming down to investigate.

Von Thoma did some quick thinking. Even in the poor light, the pilot would spot they weren't Americans. Their camouflaged uniforms stuck out like a sore thumb. What would he do about the fact? It was clear that he wouldn't attack them just to be on the safe side. He hadn't the means to do so; the spotter planes were normally unarmed. But the pilot would carry a radio. He might well report their presence if he thought they were suspicious. Hastily he knocked down Schulze's British sten gun as he raised it to take aim. At that height and speed, the *Ami* plane was a perfect target. "No firing," he commanded hastily. "Wave."

"What?"

"You heard me. Wave as if your lives depended upon it. You heard me, men – WAVE . . . Damn your eyes!"

For what seemed an age the plane buzzed them. They could see the pilot leaning out of the side panel of his cockpit quite clearly. Then, when von Thoma was beginning to think they hadn't fooled him, the artillery observer waved back cheerfully. Next instant, he had pulled back his stick and the little plane was rising. Moments later it was rapidy becoming a dark speck on the horizon. They were safe for a little while longer.

Schulze dabbed his red face. "I thought the clock was in the pisspot that time, sir," he growled.

Von Thoma wasn't listening, for suddenly he was assailed by an alarming thought. Before the Grand Duchess could continue with his briefing, he blurted out, "*Gnädiges Fraulein*, do you realise that if the *Amis* catch you, dressed in mufti as you are, they'll shoot you out of hand as a spy." He looked hard at her smiling, so honest-looking face, as if willing her to lose that smile and experience some of the doubts that he was having.

In the event he was disappointed. She didn't lose her smile. Instead she said brightly, as if it was a matter of no great importance, "Oh yes, Captain, I've known that kind of thing for years now." She shrugged easily. "I suppose in the end that's what will happen to me . . . perhaps to us all." Her voice sharpened. "But let's not waste time on such gloomy thoughts. Let's get on with the briefing . . ."

*   *   *

Perhaps some dozen miles or so away, somewhere outside the grimy Lorraine industrial town of St Avold, Hairless Harry had plenty of time to waste, while, inside the HQ of the line regiment to which they had been brought once they had crossed into US-held territory, Major Savage was de-briefed. He had Petra clasped in what he always called to his buddies, 'Old Harry's half-Nelson'. By this he meant, as he would have put it, 'one hand on her tit, giving her a sly feel and the other hand on her ass so that she can't run away and at the same time, guys, letting her know that you're in love with her.'

Of course it was difficult, due to the fact that the big French whore's vocabulary in English was limited to 'you like ficki-ficki', 'yessir' and 'how much'. So far while he had exerted all his considerable strength to massage the huge woman's bodily parts in Harry's half-Nelson, he hadn't got too far with her and her limited choice of English hadn't helped much either. For as always Hairless Harry was broke. He might have liked the 'ficki-ficki' part of her message, but the 'how much' was beyond his means. As he kept telling her somewhat desperately by now. "I just don't have the wherewithal, baby. But, honey, if you give me credit, I'll make yer eyes pop with what I've got in my britches."

But the 'offer that no woman can refuse', did not seem to be very effective with Petra, who kept protesting she didn't mind performing for money (she made that continental gesture of counting money with her finger and thumb to convey her meaning well enough), but she was really "in love with that poor dear boy, Mr Pissover – although he has a funny name."

One of the difficulties of the Harry's half-Nelson hold was the freeing of one hand to continue further. "I mean you've gotta get down to basics some time," as Hairless would explain the dilemma to his cronies. "A dame wants action not just loving-up. So guys," and here he would always throw up his huge muscular shoulders in a gesture that could have meant anything, "how are ya going get yer paws on her love-machine?" So it was now. Dare he risk taking his hand from her buttock, or from her breast in order to grope ever further in his search for final consummation? It was a problem that he still had not solved when Savage had come to the crux of his personal problem of another kind with the intelligence officer of the regiment to which they had been directed once they had crossed into Third Army territory. "So, Major," he said, considering his words carefully, "it appears to us that the Krauts are going to attack us in great strength in the north – Hodges' First Army."

Major Aronson was one of those careful, clever-faced Jews, who have something of the frail-looking academic about them, but are in reality as tough as nails. He was totally unlike the usual intelligence officers that Savage had come in contact with since he had received his 'greetings' from the President of the United States and been invited to join the Army back in '42. He was neither a 'Nervous Nelly', who saw gloom and disaster on all sides, nor one of those hail-fellow-well-met blusterers who pooh-poohed all problems.

Aronson had obviously considered carefully what he had just heard for he said, after Savage was finished, "It is a strong possibility, Major Savage. Pity that *Standartenführer* Gross succumbed to his wounds. I would have liked to pump him in some detail."

"There's something else," Savage said a little uncertainly, wondering if he was going too far. Outside he could hear Hairless Harry saying plaintively, "Come on, babe, shoot the works for old Hairless. Who knows I might not be here this time next week . . . Make an old soldier happy, honey."

Savage grinned in spite of the seriousness of the situation. Old Hairless, if he knew him at all, was going to survive a very long time yet, but for once Major Savage was wrong. His grin vanished and he said, "We think – we don't know – that the Krauts are going to make an attempt to assassinate General Patton before the trouble starts."

"Bump him off!" the idiom of the '30s gangster movie seemed incongruous in the present circumstances, but Savage could see Major Aronson was deadly serious.

"Yes, that's our impression. It would fit in, of course, with the Kraut plans for the whole op."

"How do you mean, Savage?"

But before the latter could answer, sudden chaos erupted in the farmyard HQ. Someone started to sound the hand-operated klaxon. The cook began to slam the iron bar around his triangle, but instead of the usual cry of "Come and get it," he yelled urgently, "Alarm . . . alarm . . . stand to, guys." Petra *die Peitsche* cried, "Hand off my tit, pig . . . I must get to my beloved, my darling Pissover." Savage's heart sank, as in an instant men were running everywhere, shouting and jostling, grabbing for their helmets and equipment. Somewhere, a little way off, an American machine gun began to chatter like an irate woodpecker. Christ, he told himself, *it's started already*.

Three

The big glider came swishing in through the flying snow, its pilot desperately trying to slow it up before it hit the runway. On all sides there were stabs of wild scarlet flame, mingled with the whiteout. Here and there parachutists could be glimpsed dropping or already on the ground, fighting their chutes which were dragging them across the field. Others were already advancing, firing from the hip, with here and there a flame-thrower operator firing roaring, scorching bursts from his terrible weapon, the snowfield burning, melting, hissing like a live thing in front of him. All was purposeful, deadly confusion.

The glider hit the deck, bounced, rose fifty metres and came down again. At a hundred kilometres an hour it raced down the runway, trailing a great white plume of snow behind it. Bits and pieces of the fuselage began to fall off under the tremendous impact. The wire wrapped around its tracks to give it more braking power snapped like twine. It hit an obstruction. The left wing was ripped off like the wing of some delicate dragonfly. The big glider, packed with heavily armed paras, slithered crazily to the right. Madly, the pilot, sweating and cursing fought to keep the glider under control. To no avail! It skidded off the runway. The cockpit was on its side. Great rents were torn in its canvas. Still it continued its crazy progress, ploughing through mud and snow, its wake reaching up to twenty metres. Inside the paras, battered from side to side, ripped furiously at the canvas with their knives. They wanted out.

The end came. The cockpit slammed into a petrol bowser parked beyond the little American military field's control tower. It came to an instant stop, the pilot slumped over the shattered controls, a metal spar thrust through his heart.

"*Heraus*," *Oberleutnant* Jaeger of the Sixth Parachute Regiment's 'Death or Glory' company bellowed above the sudden roar of flames from the shattered petrol bowser. "*Los . . . hopp, hopp, Männer!*" They needed no urging. Already they could smell the cloying stench of escaping petrol.

Frantically they ripped apart the wooden frame and canvas, making holes big enough for them to escape. Not a moment too soon. As the veterans of Holland and Crete flung themselves free into the melting snow outside, pelting for cover, the petrol bowser exploded.

"*Shit on shingle!*" Jaeger cursed and reeled back, hands in front of his broad, tough face, as the sea of flaming petrol flooded the area of the wrecked glider. One moment later, it, too, was burning furiously. Jaeger, running and readying his weapon at the same time, rejoicing in the utter confusion of the *Amis*, glimpsed through the flying snow, spotted a man in his underwear racing in a jeep across the tarmac. He laughed uproariously. All tension forgotten, he ripped off a burst from the hip. "*Try that on for size, Yank!*" he cried, carried away by the crazy confidence of combat.

The American rose from the seat, carried upwards by the impact of that terrible burst of fire at such close range. As he fell back, blood jetting from the line of holes in his long johns, the jeep smashed into a petrol pump. The two exploded in an instant. Cherry-red flame swamped the observation planes lined up next to the pump and they burnt like children's wooden toys. The lieutenant laughed madly and crying, "*Arses up and heil America!*" ran on.

Up in the besieged control tower, a brave young pilot died, still firing signal flares to summon rescuers who would never come. Inside a portly, bespectacled major, with the wings of a World War One flier on his fat chest, cried over and over into a dead phone, "The Krauts are here in force . . . I say, the Krauts are here in force. *Do you read me?*" A bullet struck him. He went down, still clutching the phone in his pudgy hand. His last words, as he laid his head down to one side, almost gently, as if he were going to take a little nap, were "Do you read—"

They did. Everywhere in the Nancy area, panic had broken out on this late afternoon. In the headquarters of the Third Army itself, staff officers strode back and forth anxiously, telephones jingled, red-faced noncoms bellowed. Just off the corridor a pudgy colonel, chewing at the end of an unlit cigar, was crying over the phone, "But you've got to get me the provost marshal . . . you've got to, goddamnit!"

Outside jeep drivers grunned their engines, like highly trained, nervous racing dogs straining to be let off the leash. Officers shouted orders. Clerks, cooks and couriers, who had never touched a weapon since basic training were grabbing the MIs the sergeants were throwing at them, well-fed faces aghast; while a tough, bow-legged regular cried scornfully over the confused noise everywhere, "Yeah, cream yer skivvies if ya like, you bunch of creampuff faggots . . . but ya gonna have to earn ya pay this day!"

Up in her cubbyhole of an office, Major Hartmann listened and watched gleefully, watching the 'Jewboys', as she called them mentally, running back and forth apparently in panic, telling herself, 'Yeah, Yid, now you'll see what real Aryan men can do.' Pfc Jordan burst into the office, without knocking. His face was ashen and his steel-rimmed GI glasses were steamed up a little. Obviously he was on the verge of tears under the unaccustomed steel helmet that was too big for him, "Ma'am, ma'am," he cried without saluting, "they've given me this." He held up the grease gun in abject horror. "They're expecting me to use it too . . . Ma'am," the tears were flowing openly down his pale cheeks now, "can't you do something – *anything* – please."

She looked at him contemptuously. Her answer was a jerk of her big thumb indicating the mêlée in the corridor, "On your way, buster. OUT!"

Blindly Pfc Jordan stumbled back the way he had come to be submerged in the sea of olive drab, while Major Hartmann settled back in her seat, legs spread to reveal the full glory of her drooping khaki drawers to wait for the time when she, too, would have to act . . .

Now in Nancy itself the air-raid sirens had started to sound their shrill warning. In an instant the city, which usually lived its life behind closed doors and shuttered windows during the hours of curfew sprang into frantic, pulsating activity. As the first searchlights began to part the sky above the eighteenth-century *Place Stanislas* with their silver fingers, MPs, harassed and in a great hurry, toured the streets in their jeeps calling through their loudhailers at the blank fronts of the brothels, "Hear this . . . hear this . . . This is an emergency . . . All men on furlough from the 80th Infantry . . . 26th . . . Fifth Armored . . . report to asembly area . . ." Whores, some half-naked, despite the cold, ran back and forth, screaming for their money from the GI clients, as they struggled outside into the cold winter's night. Others, drunk for the most part already, pushed their bellies forward provocatively at the MPs and sighed, "You wanna a good time, Joe . . . I kiss French . . ." One, beside herself with rage for some reason known only to herself, threw open the shutters of her cramped bedroom and flung the contenta of a tin chamber pot at the nearest jeep with a *"Salaud . . . sale con americain—"* and she didn't miss.

And as had happened twice before in the last half a decade,

179

the shabby undernourished civilians, those who had no black market connections and were not whores, started to trail from the city with their pathetic bits and pieces laden on prams, dog carts, buggies – anything with wheels. The great trek of '40 was being re-enacted this December when everyone had thought thc terrible war was about over.

"Grossartig . . . great," the Grand Duchess enthused excitedly as they drove carefully down the D road, watching the lights blazing on the *route nationale* on both sides of their little convoy heading west. The panic-stricken Yank truck drivers, trying to get away from Nancy or taking their cargoes of leave men back to the front, had torn off their blackout shields and were driving with their headlights full on. For her it was indication enough. The surprise paradrop had panicked the *Amis* totally.

Von Thoma, sitting next to her in the captured half-track, wasn't so convinced, yet at the same time he was carried away by her bubbling personality, her total conviction that nothing would go wrong. "All the same," he warned. "We've got to take care that we don't bump into an Ami roadblock unexpectedly. We've got to be prepared for instant action."

She laughed, ignoring the snow which was seeping through the holed canvas top of the vehicle. "Your boys look to me as if they're always ready for instant action." She fluttered her eyelashes in the green light reflected from the dash.

"But not from her sort," Sergeant Schulze growled in a surly fashion. But his rancour was only feigned. Like the rest of von Thoma's old hares, he was still under the sway of this beautiful lesbian who seemed to have no fear and was prepared to stick it out in the line, with all its risks of sudden death.

Oberleutnant Jaeger had not wasted a minute after the surprise assault on the little airfield had succeeded. He and his men had shot up the place, wrecking as many planes as they could with their thermite grenades, sending the surviving ground crews scurrying wildly for their underground shelters, leaving the attackers to pick up whatever vehicles were available for the next stage of their advance towards Nancy.

Now the company was bowling along at a fine speed along the *Route Nationale 74* in half a dozen captured jeeps, a two-and-a-half-ton truck belonging to the Red Ball Express and a fire tender, an exuberant 'hunter from the sky', carried away by the wild craziness of combat, ringing its bell madly, chuckling as if this were some great schoolboy jape.

It was that ringing bell which attracted the attention of Savage's force heading also towards Nancy just as they had turned off the parallel D 194 at the shelled hamlet of Varangeville to try to dodge the speeding convoys leaving the Lorraine capital at top speed. Somehow that bell, together with the intermittent shrieks of the tender's klaxon, cut through the roar of the engines, the angry snap-and-crack of the fire-fight at the airfield, as the panicked ground crews fired at each other, and the hiss and hush of exploding flares that were shooting into the night sky in crazy profusion everywhere.

Hairless Harry, who had been supporting Petra's enormous bulk in the back of the swaying, clumsy *gazogene* (naturally by gripping her wonderful flanks in his big paws), cocked his head to one side and yelled to Savage sitting next to the driver in the cab, "What d'ya make of that, sir. Them ain't the bells of St Mary's celebrating Christmas, I'm a-thinking."

"You're right there, Hairless," Savage agreed grimly, also becoming aware of the strange sound. He flung up his binoculars and focused them on the little convoy running parallel to them some five hundred yards away.

The line of vehicles moving along the main road slid into the gleaming circles of glass of his binoculars. They were American all right and they were moving towards Nancy. But why in Sam Hill's name were they sounding that goddam bell? He ran the field glasses the length of the line of the convoy until he came to the boxlike fire tender with its ladders perched on the turntable at the back. A man was standing on the running board sounding a bell. He couldn't make it out too well even in the silver light of a falling flare. But he seemed like an American. The helmet looked right and, as far as he could see, the uniform as well. He stopped short. Hurriedly he focused the glasses and peered at the coat which the man ringing the bell was wearing, trying frantically to remember where he had seen something like it before. Then he remembered – *St Lo*! That desperate street battle in which no quarter was given or expected between the Rangers and the men of the German Fifth Parachute Division. The man was wearing a long smock-like affair that reached almost to his knees – the same kind of smock the handful of wounded survivors they had finally taken prisoner at the French town had been wearing. "Christ Almighty," he exclaimed in surprise and almost dropped the glasses, "they're Krauts!"

Four

Her mind was elsewhere. The Grand Duchess knew how
to pace her mind processes. Nothing could be done
now till they reached the Cowboy General's HQ. So why
bother about it? Let the mind concern itself with something
relatively harmless, say in the past; anything but the matter of
the moment. It was an old trick she had been taught before the
war in order to fool the newly invented *Ami* lie-detector test.

So she thought of the ugly President's wife, all bosom and
good works, splattering spittle over everybody through those
awful protruding teeth of hers whenever she spoke, which was
often and for most of the time: a compulsive talker who hated
silences perhaps because they allowed her to brood. And, the
Grand Duchess told herself without any real pity, Mrs Roosevelt,
ugly, opinionated and loveless, had a lot to brood about. Perhaps
that was why she had turned to women; they loved to gossip
endlessly about their bad luck in their choice of husband and the
unhappy life to which Fate had condemned them.

She grinned and wondered yet again why women didn't
enjoy themselves. What was stopping them from taking
Fate into their own hands and shaping it any way they
wanted? Yet once she had established contact with the
First Lady back in '40 just as her boss, 'Father Christmas'
(whom she suspected was 'warm'* himself) had wanted,

* German slang for homosexual.

183

Mrs Roosevelt had been like a blushing virgin, holding her hands in front of 'it' as if she was about to lose her cherry.

It had been no different with that ugly small town dope Hartmann, with all that anti-Semitic racial purity crap of hers. The Grand Duchess shook her pretty head as if in disbelief.

"Penny for them?" von Thoma asked, cupping his hands above the noise of the racing motors.

She blinked and came back to the present. "Not worth it, *Herr Hauptmann*. You know what kind of birdbrains we poor helpless women are."

"Problems then?" he tried a new tack but, before she could reply, the sudden burst of machine-gun fire to their rear made him forget all interest in what might have been going on in that 'birdbrain' of hers.

He swung round. To their rear, a puffing-and-panting *gazogene* of French origin, followed by American jeeps, was closing the gap between it and another small convoy crawling along the main road, some five hundred metres away, slowing down by the instant as it headed for a roadblock. White tracer zipped lethally across the intervening distance and at the roadblock, the khaki-clad figures with the white-painted helmets of US 'snowdrops'* were going to ground and preparing to open fire too. "Heaven, arse and cloudburst!" he cried, flinging up his glasses, "I think it's those para boys of *Oberleutnant* Jaeger, you mentioned. The diversion." Hastily he focused the glasses.

"Yes," she said without any apparent emotion, though both of them could see without the aid of binoculars, the line of the

---

* American military policemen, named thus by continental Europeans on account of their white-painted helmets.

Sherman tanks trundling up to the rear of Jaeger's convoy. "It looks like it."

Von Thoma focused his glasses on the scene slightly above them on the raised *Route Nationale*. Jaeger's drivers were slowing down. There was nothing else they could do. They were trapped between the barricade, from which now came sporadic smalls-arms fire and the Shermans. He flashed a look at the four tanks. The commanders were already battening down their turrets. The gunners swung round their big 75mm cannon like the snouts of predatory monsters seeking out their prey. The *Ami* tanks were preparing for action too.

Desperately von Thoma sought for some way out for Jaeger's hunters from the sky. Where could they abandon their vehicles and go it on foot? Paras were used to this kind of thing; they were a lot better at it than the poor bloody infantry. They'd get back to friendly lines under their own steam.

But it seemed the paras were out of luck. The road on both sides was bordered by a deep drainage ditch with thick hedges beyond. They'd never get across that ditch and through the hedge with their vehicles. Even if they abandoned their wheels, they'd be at the mercy of the *Amis* for far too long, as they scrambled up the ditch in the open and then through the hedge. Suddenly the bell of the fire tender ceased tolling. The young para pulling the bell pitched abruptly forward, dead before he hit the white-covered *pavé*.

Von Thoma let the glasses drop to his chest. "We've got to do something,' he yelled, as the road erupted into a vicious little battle, and Jaeger's vehicles skidded and slipped to a stop at crazy angles.

"What?" she cried.

"Help him, of course. Make a distraction." He opened his mouth to yell an order to Schulze.

She caught his arm and pressed hard before he could do so.

185

He was surprised at her strength; she really hurt him. "Stop, you fool. *Biste meschugge* – are you crazy?"

"What do you shitting well mean?" he cried back hotly.

"If you have your men open fire, you draw attention to us. We can't afford that."

"I know that. But we can't just let the paras be wiped out like—" his words were drowned by the angry rat-tat of one of the Sherman's turret machine gunners opening fire. The last vehicle of Jaeger's column – the fire tender – was riddled. Its tyres exploded and a great cloud of white steam erupted from its engine.

"Our mission is most important!" she yelled. "Everything else is subordinate to that."

He stared aghast at her face. It did not look so pretty any more. The lines of laughter had suddenly grown hard and ruthless. The icy look in those light-blue eyes of hers could have frozen the recipient. Suddenly von Thoma realised why the *Abwehr* had chosen her for the job. It wasn't just the fact she was a lesbian and had used her sex to subborn the American woman officer and others, too, for all he knew. Father Christmas, as she called the head of the German secret service, had picked her because she was completely amoral, totally without scruples. "You're going to sacrifice them," he gasped, shocked.

"Of course I fucking am," she snarled. "What do you think . . . Besides it's too late how. They're trapped. They'll serve the purpose of making the stupid *Amis* believe it was they who were out to murder Patton. We'll slip through now – nice and easy. Look!" She pointed to where Jaeger's convoy was completely stalled now, with little fugures dropping out of their vehicles, some already blazing away as the tank gunners riddled them with incendiary bullets. Here and there bold, desperate paras attempted to rush the barricade on foot. They didn't get far. The MPs, well placed behind their defences, picked them off with impunity so that the survivors, desperate, panicked, milled around in an attempt to find a way out of the trap. But there was none.

"Well," she demanded angrily, her eyes flashing fire now, "what are you going to do, von Thoma? Piss or get off the pot—" Her words were drowned by the boom of the first mortar shell exploding right in the midst of the *Fallschirmjäger*. Jaeger's men fell screaming on all sides, turning the smoking snow into a red star coloured by their blood.

Von Thoma swallowed, sickened. There was no hope for the trapped survivors now. His shoulders bowed in defeat. Wordlessly, he slapped his driver over the shoulder. It was the signal to move on. Behind him Schulze said, murder in his voice now, "It ain't shitting right, yer know, mates . . . Not right at all . . ." Moments later they had vanished into the blood-red night, leaving the survivors of Jaeger's paras to be picked off by the tankers and American MPs one by one, as if the Americans were back home enjoying themselves at some backwoods fall turkey-shoot . . .

"Holy shit!" Hairless Harry exclaimed, as the convoy stopped and the Rangers fell stiffly to the scuffed snow to view that ghastly tableau of sudden death, outlined a stark harsh white by the Shermans" turret searchlights. "The Krauts didn't stand a chance."

Major Savage nodded numbly, momentarily at a loss for words. He stared at a young German, whose flesh had been stripped from the arm so that bone gleamed through it like polished ivory. God, he didn't look a day older than sixteen and now he was dead, killed in this arsehole of the world. He probably hadn't known the place's name even.

"What's the drill, Major?" Hairless Harry asked, breaking into his silent reverie, as the MPs advanced cautiously from behind their barricade, bodies bent as if against a stormy wind, coming to take a look at their deadly handiwork. "D'ya think this is the end of it, sir?"

It seemed to take the sharp-faced major with the intelligent eyes a long time to respond. Finally he said in a low, considered voice, as if he had been thinking seriously about Harry's question, "Yes and no. You can see those poor jerks were the ones who dropped at the airfield. The uniform tells yer they were airborne."

Hairless Harry nodded. To his rear, Petra *die Peitsche* was conforting a confused Peover, stroking his head and saying soothingly in French, which he didn't really understand, "Soon we shall have you in a nice warm hospital, my little cabbage. Never fear. Petra – kind auntie Petra – will see you are all right." Harry gritted his teeth, but didn't comment. Mentally, however, he promised himself that Pissover would be on kitchen duty till the day he was separated from the service if he had any say in it.

"But they were just a feint, in my opinion!" Savage was saying. "The real would-be killers are still in business."

Hairless Harry whistled softly through his teeth, Petra and Pissover momentarily forgotten. "Ya don't say, Major, but where are they in God's name?" He flungout a big paw to embrace that wild dark landscape, with the sirens still wailing their dire warning over the spiked silhouette of Nancy in the distance. "They could be anywhere – everywhere – sir. Jesus H, Major," he snorted in exasperation. "This is a real ball-cruncher."

"No it isn't," Savage answered quietly, as the MPs, outlined starkly by the harsh lights of the Shermans, began to turn over the Germans with the toes of their boots to see if they were dead. "There's going to be one place where we'll definitely find the Krauts. That's for sure."

"Where, Major?"

"They've come to get General Patton, haven't they?"

Hairless Harry whistled again. "Gotcha, Major," he said. "It takes a college education to figure out something like that," he added enviously. "Me, I left in sixth grade."

Savage didn't comment. There was no time. "'Kay, Harry," he snapped. "Let's roll 'em, tootsweet."

"Sir." Hairless Harry turned to carry out the CO's order and groaned at the sight which confronted him as he did so. Tenderly Petra had placed the wounded Pissover's head between her enormous breasts, loosening her bra so that they had free flow to form a kind of fleshy pillow for her hero, muttering softly like a mother to a beloved child. "Now you rest yourself there, *mon petit chou*. Mommi'll take care of her little darling."

Hairless Harry couldn't understand the words, but he could comprehend the gestures. He clenched a fist like a small ham and cursed under his breath like a man tried beyond all measure, as he thought of those tits being wasted in this manner on Pissover of all people. "Goddamit, it's more than a red-blooded American male can stand . . ."

Some three and a half miles away, seated calmly in the midst of all that fear and confusion, Major Hartmann perched her fat bottom on the office chair and told herself that these men, even the highest-ranking of them, were running around like a bunch of headless chickens. Only men could get themselves into a panic like that. She grinned at her own image in the mirror opposite maliciously. "Well," she said half-aloud, her decision now made – in five minutes she'd move – "be prepared for a real panic, gents." And with that she lit the small black cheroot of the type she favoured, and savoured the taste of the smoke as she sucked it down. *Time had about run out for General George S. Patton . . .*

Five

P atton raged. He strode back and forth in his pyjamas, while his black soldier valet followed, trying to calm him down with, "Now, General we don't want to get our blood pressure up, do we? We know what the surgeon-general said about your cigars, sir."

Patton tore the big unlit cigar out from between his thin lips and snarled, "The surgeon-general and my blood pressure can go to hell. *He* doesn't have to command a goddam army like I have—" He stopped short. Cocking his head to one side, trying to ignore the noise made by his panicked staff officers elsewhere in the building, he listened hard before saying, "At least the bastards are not firing at each other any more. The shooting seems to have stopped."

"Yessir, general," his negro servant, who had served him faithfully for so long agreed, chancing a white-toothed smile. "It's all over now. What about a bourbon, sir, and then go and get some shuteye—"

He didn't finish, for Codman, looking very dishevelled for that so correct Bostonian, pushed into the room with a swift knock on the door, "Sorry to interrupt you like this, general, but—"

"Where's the fire, Charley?" Patton snapped, not letting him finish in his haste to find out what was going on.

"It seems about extinguished, sir," Codman answered in a weak attempt at humour.

"Don't bullshit me, Codman," Patton said haughtily. "I might be old, but I'm not dumb. Something's going on, isn't it? What does Intelligence say?"

Codman hesitated.

"C'mon, Charley, piss or get off the pot," Patton said crudely. His negro servant looked shocked.

"Well, this is only conjectural, sir. But we think it's all an attempt on your life, General."

"The hell, you say!" Patton showed no sign of fear, just surprise; then he grew thoughtful, "But it figures. Ever since that business with the Polack and the Spitfire. Go on."

"Savage broke off his mission, sir, got through to our lines and he had some vague information that indicated an assassination was on the cards. Now the Jerries have dropped these paratroopers on the airfield and from the prisoners we've taken and questioned, it is clear that they're out to get you."

"But why now?" Patton exclaimed. "I've been fighting the bastards since November 1942 back in North Africa. Why two years later specifically here in this goddam asshole of a . . ." He let his words trail away to nothing, while the other two watched him, obviously wondering why. He could have told them, but he didn't. Instead he told himself the answer to his own question. The Krauts want to kill me *now* because they know of the trick Ike is going to pull on them or because they have learned that my Third will have to move north to face up to the new German *surprise* offensive when it comes. "Holy cow," he exclaimed at last and Codman said hurriedly, "Something the matter, sir?"

"You can bet your goddam life that something is the matter, Charles," Patton yelled, his thin sunken cheeks flushing dramatically. Before Codman had time to ask any further questions, Patton started to rap out orders, as if his very life depended upon them, which, in a way, it did. "Get Savage here at the double," he cried. "I want to question

191

him personally. "Those Kraut POWs the MPs took as well
. . . Any new German prisoners the guards make, I want to
see them in double quick time also—"

"May I ask, sir," Codman gasped, taking down his master's
commands as fast as he could, "why all the urgency?"

"You may not," Patton answered, while behind his man-
servant scratched his close-cropped greying hair and told
himself, he'd always known the master was slightly crazy,
not like other men, but now he'd gone completely mad. "But
I'll tell you this for free, Charley. This is a matter of the
greatest national importance. If anyone fucks this one up, I'll
personally castrate him with a blunt knife – *slowly*, understood.
Now get to it."

Codman fled . . .

With von Thoma and the Grand Duchess in the lead, the
L-Squad troopers slipped down the ancient streets through
the shadows like the seasoned veterans they were. Von
Thoma had ordered them to muffle their boots with their
spare pairs of socks. Now they moved noiselessly, every
man tense and alert, ears atuned to the noise and shouts
all around them, ready to spring into action at a moment's
notice.

Von Thoma didn't like the assignment one bit, or their guide
the Grand Duchess but he had to admire the thoroughness of
Skorzeny's plan and the expertness of their guide. She knew
the route they had to take as if she had walked it all her life
which, he knew, was impossible. She had learned it long ago
by heart. So far she hadn't made a single slip-up.

Now they were getting ever closer to Patton's HQ, and
von Thoma knew that the chances were they would soon
bump into trouble. Normally around army HQs there were
troops billeted everywhere. It would take only one suspicious
Ami to challenge and, as Schulze would have put it in his

own inimitable way, 'The tick-tock would really be in the pisspot then.'

Time passed leadenly. The searchlights had ceased probing the sky, now that the MPs had dealt with the threat of Jaeger's paras, but a thin cold sickle moon had slipped from behind the ragged clouds and was illuminating the cobbled streets of the old quarter. Above them on the heights, it shone on the snow-capped hills. Romantic but highly lethal, von Thoma told himself in the same instant that the challenge came which he had been dreading all along. *"Halt—"* the command died on the lips of the soldier who had stepped out of the shadows to challenge; Schulze's knife was protruding, as if by magic, from his skinny chest. The sentry's legs gave beneath him like those of a new-born calf. His rifle fell from his suddenly nerveless fingers and tumbled to to the ground. A moment later he followed before they had a chance to lower him gently and noiselessly.

The sound was enough, it alerted yet another sentry. He, too, came out of the shadow. This time he had his rifle tucked to his right hip. Even before he challenged, he fired. Flame stabbed the gloom. A slug howled off the wall just above the Grand Duchess's head. She yelled something very unducal-like.

One of von Thoma's men reacted instinctively *'Phut!'* His silenced pistol spat fire. The American went down on his knees fighting off death, blood spurting in an arc from the gaping wound in his chest. Schulze didn't give him a chance. He kicked him in his contorted face. The cruelly shod boot caught him under his upraised chin. Something snapped like a twig underfoot in a bone-dry summer wood. He went down without another sound.

But that single rifle shot had done it. There were cries on all sides. "Over here guys," someone cried urgently.

"After me," the Grand Duchess hissed. "Keep close *Los.*"

They needed no urging. There was the sound of running feet

everywhere among the shabby unpainted eighteenth-century houses. Almost noiselessly in their stockinged feet, they followed the lady, slipping in and out of alleys and narrow lanes. Still they simply couldn't shake off their pursuers. There were too many of them. When one bunch gave up, another took up the chase. Twice they had almost been taken and they had only managed to dodge the *Amis* at the very last minute; and twice an anxious von Thoma had gasped to the woman, his face lathered with sweat despite the bitter cold, "We've got to find cover before it's too late," to which she had replied with contemptuous superiority, "Leave it to this poor woman, *Herr Hauptmann*, she'll save your precious hide, don't worry." The second time he had been tempted to strike her. But he had caught himself in time, for now he knew that for the moment at least, their fate lay in her hands.

Somewhere a clock boomed midnight as she said, pointing through the snow which was coming down hard now at a large square building to their front, "Patton's HQ in the *Rue Auxerre*. We're over there to the right of it. Their yards connect. That's why Father Christmas picked it in the first place."

"Is it safe?" he began, but before he could complete his question, there was the sound of rubber-soled GI boots running and squelching over the new snow and a voice crying excitedly, "Over here, guys. I've picked up their trail." They pelted on . . .

Major Hartmann took a deep breath, glanced at her pudgy hands – they were rock-steady – and rose confidently from her office chair. It was time for her to carry out her part of the plan. Then, as an afterthought she took the little, pearl-handled .22 out of the drawer. One never knew. Hiding in the darkness, Pfc Jordan watched her stride out of the office, tucking the pistol into the waistband of her skirt. He frowned puzzled. What was the old butch dame up to? Even his urgent need to keep himself away from some officious NCO who might want to recruit him into a makeshift fighting force couldn't quite kill his curiosity. Hardly aware he was doing so, he hefted up his MI and followed . . .

"This is it," the Grand Duchess panted, as they closed the great leather-covered, padded door behind them, deadening the sounds and shouts from the old quarter all about them.

Von Thoma blinked. The blackout wasn't up so after a moment he could see the interior of the dusty old hall, which smelled of dust, neglect and a sharp odour which made his nose twitch and which he couldn't identify. 'What is this place?" he asked, as the sound of running feet outside disappeared into the distance.

She laughed softly, a strange sound in that uncanny remote building. "Somewhere where your ordinary Otto Normal Citizen* wouldn't venture, especially at night. Look over there to your right!"

He followed the direction of her outstretched hand and swallowed hard. A huge peeling oil painting dominated the flaking wall, yellow with age. It depicted a frock-coated surgeon with what looked like a scalpel in a dirty hand towering above a naked male, with his arms tied behind his knees so that the whole of his bare underbody was presented to the grinning surgeon. Next to him there there was a hunchback with a beard, also grinning fiendishly, with a stopwatch in his hand. At his misshapen feet there was a bowl and a jug. The jug was full of blood. "What in three devils" name was going on there?" Von Thoma choked, already wishing he hadn't asked.

Calmly, that cocky knowing grin on her face once more, as a heavy yet somehow pregnant silence descended upon the

* Translation of the German *Otto Normalverbraucher*, i.e. 'John Smith', 'Joe Blow', etc.

building, the Duchess explained. "The bound man is suffering from bladder stones. The surgeon just filled his bladder with barley water to distend it. Soon he's going to open the bladder with that scalpel, tear it open further with his fingers and then chip out the stones. The dwarf is going to time him. If the whole op takes more than a minute, the patient will die – hence the stopwatch." She paused and delivered the punchline with relish, as if enjoying herself. "Naturally all without drugs."

Schulze just behind von Thoma said thickly. "Poor shit."

"Poor shit, indeed," she agreed calmly and indicated the bottles. "Bits and piece of other poor shits who didn't make it. Most of them didn't."

Schulze averted his gaze quickly, muttering he'd seen better things at "the bottom of a pisspot or puking-jar in the pox hospital."

She laughed softly. "So you can see why we should be left strictly alone in here."

Von Thoma took his eyes off the horrible-looking specimens in the jars filled with pickling fluid, a hundred years or so of human misery preserved for ever for the benefit of medical students who never came to this place any more. For he could see from the centimetre-deep dust on the tiled floor that no one had entered it for a long time. "How long?" he asked, eager to be out of it as soon as possible.

"How long?" she repeated. "As soon as our contact in the Cowboy General's HQ switches on the lights and compromises the blackout over there. Then we move. Now gather round, the lot of you. I'll show you the lay-out of his quarters exactly. Cost what it may, *one* of us has got to finish him off." There was steel in her voice now, as with the toe of her shoe, she started to draw the plan in the dust of the floor.

Afterwards when she had asked the usual, "Any questions?" and had been rewarded with a stony silence (for in truth, even the hardened old hares such as Schulze, were awed by the atmosphere of this gruesome hiding place), she said, "Escape route. There are two US ambulances parked outside the dispensary – here." She made a mark with her foot in the dust. "They will have fuel for two hundred kilometres, have the keys in the ignition, and medical gowns, such as *Ami* doctors wear in the front seats. We use them to make our escape."

Von Thoma nodded his understanding, telling himself that the plan had been worked out very well and perhaps they stood a chance of surviving after all, and then asked, "And you, Gracious Miss?"

The irony was wasted on her now. She was tense and full of steely resolve; even her habitual cynicism seemed to have vanished. "Me?"

"Yes, will you be standing by the ambulances? I just want to know. We don't need any mix-ups at this stage of the op."

"There will be none," she pronounced, very dogmatic now. "Why?" She answered her own question. "Because I'm going with you . . . I shall be in at the kill!"

Von Thoma opened his mouth to protest, but then closed it again. She had made up her mind and when the Grand Duchess made up her mind, there was nothing that one could say to change it. He turned to his men. "All right," he said, "you can have a last smoke . . . it won't be long now."

Von Thoma watched them in that gloomy hall, as the snow fell softly outside in solid white sheets. They smoked wordlessly, hands cupped around their cigarettes, the red glimmer hollowing out their tough honest faces into death's heads. He told himself that they were about done now. The scene was set, the actors were in place and the drama could commence . . .

Six

The panic around the HQ seemed to have settled now. The air-raid sirens had just sounded the 'all clear'. In the distance, the wild shooting had virtually ceased. Now close at hand was the orderly sound of marching and the swish of tyres riding through the new snow: patrols, on foot and mounted, checking the area out. The 'flap' was about over.

Major Hartmann was pleased by the reduced noise. It would make her task and that of the German assassination squad much easier. By now she knew of the feint which had been discovered and dealt with, as had been planned in the Reich all along. The male pricks at HQ might congratulate themselves on their success, but then they didn't realise that the German L-Squad had come through scot free. They were out there at this very moment, waiting for the signal to carry out their vital mission. No one had informed her as yet what would happen to her afterwards, but through her link with the Grand Duchess she knew that the latter had stated categorically that nothing would happen to her, come what may. And she believed the Grand Duchess implicitly. After all she had a sneaking suspicion that the Grand Duchess still loved her as she had done back in what now seemed another age, in those halcyon days in Washington in the summer of 1940 when she had fallen in love and agreed (almost *demanded* would have been a better description), to work for the Grand Duchess and the cause of the 'New Order'.

For a moment as she prowled down the corridor, she allowed herself a quick vivid recall of that first night of love. How shy and bourgeois she had been in her floral nightgown next to a totally naked Grand Duchess with her tanned, trained athletic body! She had lain with her eyes closed, hardly daring to breathe, her legs tightly pressed together so that her knees had become a startling white, while the Grand Duchess had kissed her over and over again, working her greedy damp hand under the fabric to feel her big heavy breasts, the nipples sticking out like organ stops. Oh, those cunning fingers and even more cunning lips and tongue. What unrestrained, almost primeval sexual pleasure she had experienced that night! She had turned almost crazy, gasping and panting, lathered in sweat, tossing and turning, writhing upon the damp sheet until the Grand Duchess had forced her down once more and continued that exquisite torture until she had been unable to bear it any longer and had exploded in one great noisy burst of unsuppressed pleasure.

"Stop it," she ordered herself, feeling her gross body beginning to shake at the memory. "Concentrate . . . concentrate on the task ahead . . . Come on, girl, *obey!*"

Behind her in the shadows Pfc Jordan heard the whispering and told himself, 'she's going nuts . . . absolutely raving mad.' He tightened his grip on the automatic and walking on the side of his feet as he had been trained to do, he followed noiselessly, his mind racing electrically. What the Sam Hill was the bull dyke up to?

She stopped at the end of the corridor, just outside the open door of the little room. Now with the flap apparently over, the off-duty guards relaxed in the warm, smoke-filled fug of the room. A handful of them, still fully dressed, save for their helmets, lay sprawled out on their bunks, snoring loudly, getting in some 'sack time' before the Orderly Officer came round to do his nightly check. A couple of them were squatting in front of the roaring pot-bellied French stove, playing poker on an upturned ration crate. At the simple trestle table the 'orderly dog', a fat, bespectacled sergeant, was scribbling in the guardroom log, yawning all the while. It was obvious that the heat from the stove, which was now glowing a dull pink, was knocking him out. He'd be asleep like the rest in a few minutes.

Hartmann nodded her bobbed head in approval. It was just as she had hoped. They'd cause no trouble. She glanced at the row of switches, each one with a neat label under it, above the rack of Garands, neatly secured and locked in the rifle rack, of which the OD Sergeant had the key. All the guards were without weapons, save the bespectacled NCO, who carried his Colt in the leather holster at his side, the thongs tied down beneath his pudgy knee as if he were some goddam movie Western gunslinger. Her lips curled in even more contempt. Easy meat even for a single woman like herself. She drew in a deep breath and started to count off to three.

Jordan tensed. He was still very puzzled. All the same he knew that something fishy was about to happen. He clicked off the 'safety' and with hands that were suddenly damp with sweat, he took a firmer grip of his Garand.

Hartmann acted. In one and the same movement she pulled out the long tube of a grenade and flung it exactly into the centre of the little room. "What the hell?" one of the card players exclaimed shocked, as there was a soft but sharp crack and a thick jet of green smoke started to stream out of the capsule rapidly.

It was effective immediately. The guard who had shouted, took a great gulp of the gas and started choking at once, hands grabbing his throat. At the desk, the bespectacled sergeant, eyes popping behind his glasses with surprise, half rose, fumbling with the flap of his pistol holster. He never managed it. As the choking gas swept up around him, he fell face forward on to his log, choking and coughing, the vomit spewing out onto the paper.

From a safe distance, mouth pressed tight, Jordan watched in horrified fascination as Hartmann slipped on a GI gas mask from the khaki-coloured sling bag the WACs carried. What the hell? he asked himself, as she ventured into that room now filled with gas, the men on the bunks grabbing at their throats, eyes bulging from their sockets, as they choked and gurgled, trying to stave off unconsciousness, perhaps even death as far as Jordan knew.

Major Hartmann moved into the room. The other card player, legs moving jerkily as if he were in the throes of some kind of fit, tried to stop her. She brushed his hands away easily. He fell backwards and lay on the floor, fouling himself as he drifted off into unconsciousness.

She pushed by the sergeant's desk. Reaching up and ignoring the men choking and gurgling, some of them spewing a nauseating green fluid now from their riddled lungs, she felt with her big hand along the line of switches. Tense as he was, a watching Jordan wondered what the hell she was up to. Suddenly she found what she was looking for. She pulled down the switch. Inside the building little happened, but outside the perimeter lights of the HQ to be used only in an emergency if the place ever came under attack, sprang into blinding, bright-white light.

Jordan got it immediately. The big dyke was signalling to the Krauts. Perhaps with that name and her hatred of the Jews, she was a Kraut herself. What was he going to do? Already outside, whistles were being shrilled urgently and a harsh, angry official voice was crying, "Put out that fuckin" light d'ya hear . . . PUT THAT LIGHT OUT!"

Major Hartmann wasted no more time. She backed out. As an afterthought she tossed the empty gas cylinder to the floor. It made a hollow sound. The sound seemed to act as a signal for a bemused Jordan, He brought up his automatic rifle. "Hold it there!"

She stopped short. He could hear her shocked intake of breath as she became aware of him standing in the shadows, rifle at the ready. Not for long. She pulled herself together, ignoring the angry shouts at the lights from outside. "What's this, Private Jordan?" she demanded. "What in God's name are you pointing that rifle like that at me? Don't you know it's a court-martial offence to threaten an officer?"

"You're up to no good," he quavered, weakening suddenly.

"What the devil do you mean?"

"PUT THAT FRIGGIN LIGHT OUT AT ONCE" the angry voice from outside reminded him of his duty.

"You know," he said doggedly.

"Put a ma'am on that," she snapped, "remember I'm your superior officer."

"You're not . . . you're a frigging—". He couldn't quite put a name to what she was, but his resentment bubbled over all the same. "Somebody in authority ought to have a word with you."

She felt a cold finger of fear trace its way down her spine. Now it was vitally important for her to get away before the balloon really went up. She didn't want this callow fool of a youth hauling her in front of the Provost Marshal. She had to act. "Dont be a damn fool," she cried, feeling in her waistband for the little .22 pistol. "Get back to your duty station at once, private. I'm giving you a direct order to do so."

"You're not giving me an order to do—" the words froze on his lips, as she pulled out the pistol and levelled it at him menacingly.

"I'm not what?" she said coldly.

Jordan didn't answer. Suddenly he wasn't afraid. In fact, he was damned angry in an icy-cold, clinical, almost detached manner; angry as he had never been before. What right had the cow to order him around with her eternal ranting about 'niggers' and 'heebies' and 'goddam Franklin *Jewish* Rosenfeld'! Why should she order him about – she wasn't even a loyal American!

"Lower that rifle," she commanded, sure that she was fully in charge now. Outside there was the sound of hurrying feet through the snow and soft orders in German. They were here, she told herself jubilantly. They had seen her signal. Patton was as good as dead. "Come on," she urged, jerking up the muzzle of her pistol, ugly broad face exuding triumph. "Don't screw me about—"

"I'll screw you about," he interjected wildly. "You sonuvabitch. Take that!" He pressed the trigger of his Garand. The automatic erupted. The slugs ripped her upper body apart in the same moment she fired herself, slamming a bullet into his guts. He gasped with shock as her uniform shirt filled with blood, burst to reveal her white heavy breasts, peppered with holes through which the blood oozed in increasing amounts. "You bast—" she began. But the blood started to trickle down the side of her face. Her knees began to give way. In the same moment that Pfc Jordan went down on his knees like some pious communicant being called to prayer in some great Gothic cathedral, Major Hartmann slammed to the blood-stained floor, dead before she hit it.

The impact roused Jordan. He lifted his sagging head. He shook it. The red veil of unconsciousness which threatened him, disappeared. Gasping for breath as if he were running some great race, he began to crawl towards the switchboard on all fours. "Got to turn it off," he whispered to himself, ignoring his guts which were falling through the jagged gory wound in his stomach and were being dragged along with him, "Got to—"

With a hand that trembled violently, he reached upwards. It seemed to take an eternity. He blinked his eyes constantly. Desperately he tried to fight off the red fog which seemed about to blind him. "Got to," he croaked, ignoring the pool of warm steaming blood in which he knelt uncertainly. "Got . . . got . . ." His fingers felt the brass switch. He attempted to flick it down and off. To no avail. His fingers felt like soft putty. He simply didn't have the strength. "Got . . . to," he urged again, his voice come from far, far away now. The switch slipped down in the same moment that he knew he couldn't last any longer. As he fell and lay still in a pool of his own blood, the lights outside went out and the last thing that Pfc Jordan, who had been so frightened of going to the front, heard before he died was the curses in German of abruptly frustrated men.

"It's them!" Savage cried. "Those lights. *Look*!" Even as he shouted his warning, voice full of excitement at their breakthrough at last, the lights went out with abrupt suddenness. But their brief appearance had sufficed. Most of his Rangers had seen them and located their site. Hairless Harry hit the brakes. Behind him the other drivers did the same. Without orders – they weren't needed with those men blooded so long before at 'Bloody Omaha' – they dropped from their trucks. There were a few moments of hesitation, while Savage decided what to do about the wounded, including Peover, who was clamouring to go with them, despite his wound and the heavy snowfall. "All right," he yelled, his decision made, as he wiped the thick wet flakes of snow from his unshaven face, "bring them with us. You can manage, Petra?" he asked in German.

"*Klarer Fall*," she answered eagerly and began to help an embarrassed Peover out of the truck to the snide remark of an envious Hairless, who commented, "A woman like that'll need more than a hug to keep her warm on a cold night like this, Pissover." He grabbed his bulging crotch to make his meaning quite clear. Then they were off, bent low against the flying snow, blinking all the time, trying to keep their eyes clear and penetrate the solid white wall of the raging snowstorm.

Up front, carbine tucked close to his hip, Savage knew that they might well be walking straight into an ambush. But there was no other way he could do it. Speed was of the essence. He had to take risks. Urgently he called over his shoulder, "Keep moving, guys . . . no slacking . . . Just keep moving."

"In a pig's eye!" Hairless Harry growled, but no one was listening to the big noncom now. They were all too intent on what was soon to come.

Von Thoma's assault party hit trouble as soon as they rammed their vehicle through the main gate and came to an abrupt stop. Instantly a burst of tommy-gun fire raked the windscreen. Their driver slumped dead over the wheel. With the horn screeching, as if it would never stop, Schulze leaned out of the side window, peering through the snow and then let fly with a stick grenade. It burst in a flash of vivid orange light which split the white wall of snow and revealed the dramatic sight of the *Ami* with the tommy gun who had just fired at them, whirling through the air – headless. Next moment the Grand Duchess was crying at the top of her shrill voice, "*Los . . . raus vorwärts!*"

"Up yer kilt!" Schulze yelled back angrily. All the same he obeyed. He flung himself out, rolled over in the snow and came up all in one movement – blazing away with his sten gun as he did so.

Now all was controlled chaos. The assault force, with von

Thoma, the Grand Duchess and Schulze in the lead, surged forward. All of them fired as they did so. 'Marching fire' was always the best in such confused battles. The side with the greater nerve and firepower always won.

A wall loomed up. They had been expecting it. It didn't stop them for a moment. "Bend yer asses!" Schulze yelled through the flying snow.

Two men bent, clenched their hands together and waited. Not for long. The first man sprang forward up onto their clenched fists. The couple gave a heave. He grabbed for the parapet. Next instant he had scrambled over the top and disappeared at the same moment that the next candidate for sudden death, slung his weapon and charged forward.

Again they were moving forward in the courtyard with the same three in the lead. The lights might have vanished, but von Thoma and the Grand Duchess knew exactly where they wanted to be. Again there was wild firing from the upper storeys of the HQ building. It didn't bother the attackers noticeably. The defenders were obviously rattled and the raging snowstorm wasn't helping their aim much. Slugs flew everywhere, whining off the parked vehicles, ploughing up the snow, but von Thoma shouted warningly to his men, "Fire only when you spot a target." He knew they would understand. They wouldn't give their own position away unnecessarily by the tell-tale flash of a weapon being fired.

They neared the door, from which the corridor led to Patton's private quarters. The Grand Duchess hesitated. It wasn't because she was afraid. She simply didn't want her life wasted for nothing; then she was sure that someone was waiting behind that door for the first person to open it.

But von Thoma's old hares had assaulted many a defended

building in the past terrible years. They had the drill down to a fine art. Schulze poised, big boot raised. Next to him, another trooper crouched with a hand-grenade raised. To his right was a third with his Schmeisser tucked tightly to his hip. *"Ein . . . zwei . . . drei,"* he counted off the seconds. *"jetzt."* He slammed his foot against the door with all his strength. The lock gave. It flew open. The man with the grenade lobbed it in and dropped to the ground. To his right the third man flung himself against the wall as the blast, filled with flying steel shrapnel, came hurtling outwards, and ripped off a killing burst.

Even as the defenders screamed shrilly, high and hysterical like women, in their dying agony, Schulze and the others were charging through, coughing and spluttering in the choking acrid smoke, springing over the bloody bodies writhing on the floor, intent on the push forward.

"Come on, men," von Thoma yelled, carried away by the unreasoning primitive blood lust of battle. "The captain's got a hole in his ass! Follow me!"

Schulze yelled his approval, his broad face streaked with sweat and smoke. "You heard that, Gracious Miss . . . lead on!"

Grimly intent, knowing that they had merely minutes to carry out the assassination and get away, they rushed on. The Grand Duchess did, too. Her mind was racing. Something had gone wrong, despite the fact that Hartmann had switched on the outside perimeter lights as planned. Where was the ugly cunt? She should be here to guide them personally to her boss's quarters. Even as she ran with the rest, who were now tossing grenades into the offices on each side of the corridor – they kept the defenders in cover for a while – she told herself that, as always, women were a disappointment. Men were useless in bed – no comparison with women – but they were obedient creatures and above all, *reliable*! Women never. Suddenly she laughed out loud, or would have done if she had had enough breath to do so. She realised for the first time, she didn't like women either. In fact, she didn't like anyone except herself. "Christ on the Cross," she gasped, as she ran round the corner and saw the huddled figure in khaki, apparently crawling down the side of the corridor, trailing blood, "I don't like shitting anybody." That overwhelming realisation might well have stopped her dead, right in the middle of the danger coming from both sides, if she hadn't recognised the crawling figure at that moment. It was the American cow – Hartmann.

The Grand Duchess faltered in spite of herself. "What is it?" she gasped, almost stumbling over the dying WAC officer.

Hartmann looked up at her. "For God's sake, keep moving," von Thoma implored. She wasn't listening. She stared down at the ugly woman with the suspicion of a moustache and repeated her question.

Hartmann's eyelids flickered rapidly. The end of her large nose was abruptly pinched and an ivory-white: both indications that she didn't have long to live. "I knew . . . I knew," she gasped, the blood trickling a bright-frothy pink down her chin, again the Grand Duchess knew the signs – she had been shot in the lungs, "you'd . . . come."

Suddenly the Grand Duchess straightened up. There was no time for pity now. "I can't help you—" she began and gasped, as if someone had suddenly rammed a hard fist into her guts. She staggered backwards, caught completely off-guard. "What . . . what?" The next slug spun her completely round and, as she twirled crazily like the excited kid she had once been at her first dancing class, at that long forgotten *Tanzschule*, she glimpsed von Thoma.

He was on his knees, supporting himself with his hands. Large gobs of blood mingled with pale rubbery pieces of lung were falling from his gaping mouth, as he shook his head like a boxer trying not to go down for a count of ten. Then she was on her back on the floor and he had vanished. They seemed all to have vanished. But as she drifted in and out of consciousness, she knew that they were still there; she could hear their yelps of pain and cries for mercy, as the cruel firing continued, crashing back and forth in the tight confines of the corridor like claps of thunder.

She drew up her knees into her stomach to try to diminish the pain. It didn't help much, but the red fog which had threatened to overcome her seemed to vanish as a result. Now she could hear someone pleading in German – the voice seemed a long way off – "*Nicht schiessen . . . bitte nicht schiessen . . .* DONT SHOOT!" There was the crash of a shot at close by. The pleading ended suddenly, with the noise reverberating back and forth, as if it might well go on for ever.

Von Thoma heard the shot, but it didn't seem to matter. He simply lay there and waited for it to happen. It was not the way he had always expected to die, but he *had* expected to die violently. Now that time had come. In a way he didn't mind. It had been ordained thus ever since he had first marched to battle as a fresh-faced young soldier back '39 – so long ago. As the voices, angry, frightened, anguished, started to recede all about him, von Thoma knew that he couldn't let his old hares all die in this trap. "Give in, lads," he said weakly. But even as he gasped the words, his chest heaving wildly with the effort, he knew none of them heard him and even if they had, how would they escape in this crazy, confused battle of the corridor? Somehow his fingers managed to claw the pin out of his smoke grenade. Weakly he lifted his hand.

"Look out, sir," Hairless Harry yelled urgently, as he saw the movement among the dead and dying who now littered the

209

floor. He lifted his tommy gun. But he couldn't fire it. There were struggling men, German and American, everywhere. He groaned and shouted his warning again. Savage swung round. He saw von Thoma's feebly raised hand with the grenade. He fired instinctively from the hip. Von Thoma jerked back as the bullet slammed into his chest, ripping his rib cage apart, scattering bits and pieces of his flesh in a gory shower. Next instant the grenade slipped from his nerveless fingers, rolled along the floor and started to eject smoke in a thick brown stream.

The smoke filled her gaping mouth as the Grand Duchess coughed and choked like an ancient asthmatic in the throes of an attack But it had an effect. It revived her. Her pain vanished suddenly. For a few minutes she felt new strength and purpose flood through her dying body, as the smoke submerged her and the bloody carnage all around. She had to do something. What? Her brain began to work again. Of course. *That*!

Her left breast hanging out of her ripped, red blouse like a pulped apple, she started to crawl, everything else forgotten – the others, the pain, the knowledge that she was going to die soon. None of it mattered. Murder in her heart, carried away by the crazy unreasoning logic of combat, she crawled down that corridor, round the corner and staggered to the stairs where *he* was to be found . . .

ENVOI

Peace is gonna be one hell of a letdown.
General Patton 1945.

The interior of the sedan was pretty well steamed up now. All the same the young captain and Savage could see out of the car's windows. It was snowing heavily. The flakes were coming down in a solid white wall, as if they would never stop. Already the graves were capped by the softness of the snow. They looked almost pretty.

Savage took another careful sip of the bourbon and hot coffee or 'java', as the young captain called it, probably to humour him by using the long outdated wartime slang for coffee. "Make a nice Christmas card," he said. "Here rest our Glorious Dead. Happy Christmas." He chuckled throatily but the chuckle turned into a nasty cough; and besides the captain was too intent upon the story for humour. Impatiently he asked, "And what happened next, sir . . . when you rushed upstairs to General Patton's quarters?"

Discreetly Savage spat into his Kleenex and looked at the spittle. It was as he expected; there was blood in it. It wouldn't be long now, he told himself. "Well, I guess I can pass it on to somebody who might remember it before I—" He didn't complete the thought. It would spoil his revelation for the young soldier. "Well," he said, staring at the flying snow and remembering how the long-dead Pissover had loved the snow, but then he was a very proper New Englander. Hairless Harry, the Californian, who now rested next to him in Hamm and who had given him his nickname, hated the stuff. "Frigging snow,"

213

he had always snorted. "Makes you lose ya faith in frigging God for having made the frigging lousy stuff."

"What happened?" he repeated the captain's eager question. "Well, you can imagine the confusion. Down below in the corridor there was still hell going on. One of the Krauts – Excuse me, we're supposed to say 'Germans' these days, aren't we?" He gave the younger man his lopsided smile, trying not to dislodge his top set as he did so – "had shot the lights out. Naturally they were trying to do a bunk, the ones who'd survived. My guys, as you can guess, weren't too keen on that. They were shooting everything that moved. Brother, was that some Doneybrook!" He gasped for breath.

"And you?"

"I followed the dame. They called the woman the Grand Duchess. We never did find out her real name even after the war when we captured most of the *Abwehr* files. She was standing there in his bedroom, dripping blood. One of her breasts had been mangled horribly. She looked a mess and you didn't need a crystal ball to see that she was dying on the spot. But standing there in a pool of her own blood, she was still full of piss and vinegar – you know, defiant in that surly peasant manner the Krauts have." In his eagerness to depict the scene Savage forgot that he was using the forbidden word.

"Patton, now he was sitting in some kind of recliner, a book in one hand still, as if she'd surprised him reading, a Colt in the other – one of those pearl handled ones of his." He hesitated and it was only later that the captain understood why. "And he had one hell of a fresh wound in his right side. The blood was really spurting from it – a helluva lot for such an old guy." He paused and took another sip of the coffee and bourbon mix, as if it might give him strength to continue. "They were just staring at each other, not saying anything. You know, like the last scene of the final act of one of those melodramas they used to show in the movie theatres back in the '30s?"

The captain didn't know, but he nodded, as if he did and gasped, "You mean that she'd shot General Patton, sir. Wow!"

"Yes. But he was still with it. I remember he looked at me slowly, really slowly, as if it was taking all his strength for him to move his head in my direction, and croaked. 'Kill her . . . kill the bitch . . . and all the rest of 'em . . . Nobody must know.' By now he was slurring his words, head twisted to one side, as if he might have just suffered a stroke." He paused to catch his breath.

Outside now, it was snowing even harder. It was as if some god on high was trying to blot out an evil, corrupt world for ever. The snowfall was so fierce that the tombstones, including Patton's had vanished. In their places were rounded humps in a field of white like it had been in that December of '44 when the corpses of the sudden dead had disappeared, too, save for a hand or arm, frozen stiff, sticking stiffly upward as if appealing for succour and help, which would never come.

"What did *you* do, sir?" the captain asked in an awed voice, as if the snow-heavy silence was sacred and shouldn't be broken by the voices of timorous mortals.

"Do?" Savage's voice was vague, far away now. "What could I do He was dying—"

"Dying?" the captain interjected.

But Savage was no longer listening . . .

"*You*'re not going to kill me," the Grand Duchess had snarled. "You haven't got the guts." Her English was accented but fluent; he could tell, as he stood there uncertainly, she had spent a lot of time in the States. "You're all the same, you Americans—"

"Shut up, damn you!" Savage had interrupted, knowing she was right. Patton, now fighting for every breath in the chair, his Colt wavering visibly, was the exception; *he* could have killed her, but Savage guessed he no longer had the strength to do so. His eyes were already taking on that tell-tale inward look which signalled the end was approaching.

215

She looked up at him tauntingly, gasping for breath, as if she were running a great race, "Well," she challenged. "Fucking well do it, tough guy." She thrust out that shattered breast of hers, the nipple hanging loose over her stomach in a mess of red gore. "Here . . . SHOOT!"

The listening captain's mouth dropped open, but Savage was no longer aware of the young officer. His mind and imagination were back at HQ in Nancy's *Rue Auxerre* all those years before, when he had been faced with that overwhelming decision: to kill or not to kill a woman. Later he recalled the faint droning coming from outside and the first thin wail of the air-raid sirens over Nancy's *Place Stanislav*. But that had been later. Now his whole being was concentrated on the terrible choice that was being forced upon him – and him alone; for Patton was slipping down in his chair, mouth gaping open, meaningless sounds coming from it. The Grand Duchess had fallen silent too. Instead she stared up at him, still defiant, but with that raging fire quenched in her eyes now, the spirit draining from her ruined body, as if someone had opened an invisible tap. "*God Almighty*", he cursed to himself, face racked by despair and doubt, "*what in hell's name, am I going to do?*"

Outside the strange roar was getting louder and the wail of the sirens from the city's centre was approaching ever nearer. He didn't seem able to make sense of it. What did the noise signify?

Patton hawked, head twisted to one side, as if he were being strangled and he spat blood onto the floor near the dying woman. "*K—*" the first letter of that final order forming quite clearly on his blood-flecked, cracked lips.

Slowly, very very slowly, Savage raised his pistol. The Grand Duchess met his sudden look of determination steadfastly. She knew what he was going to do. But she wasn't afraid. Savage aimed. He felt the cold trickle of sweat course slowly down the small of his back. He took first pressure. His finger, crooked around the trigger, went white at the knuckle. He hesitated. Later he never quite knew why, but then perhaps he did and wanted to sublimate the reason.

"*K . . . ILL!*" the strangled command finally escaped Patton's thin lips, exploding into the tension of the room of death. He pressed the trigger and in that same moment the roof came tumbling in as the first bomb of the aerial attack which preceded the great German 'surprise' attack exploded. *Crack*! The pistol erupted. Everything went black. Savage knew no more . . .

The captain sat in stunned silence. The only sound now was the steady hum of the fan forcing hot air into the sedan to clear away the mist from the steamed-up windows. He seemed drained of emotion; too shocked to comment even. Finally, after what seemed an age, while Savage slumped beside him in the depths of the plush seat, hardly seeming to breathe, the captain rubbed the last of the steam away and peered out through the flying snow. It was as if he were trying to assure himself that Patton's grave still lay there under Old Glory hanging limp and wet from its pole.

"But sir," he asked, his voice strained and lacking that old West Point confidence and certainty, "if General Patton was killed that day, who led the Third Army during the Battle of the Bulge?" He swallowed hard, as if he were finding it difficult to speak . . . "and sir, who's buried in that grave over there, please?"

Savage didn't answer.

"Sir." The captain turned his head slowly, as if it was worked by stiff, rusty springs. "Did you hear, sir, what I asked?" He stared hard at the old general, slumped in the seat next to him. He seemed to have shrunk even more. "General Patton? – what really happened?" With a gesture of irritation, he reached out to take the old man by his skinny shoulder. He didn't make it. Slowly, very slowly, almost in slow motion, General Savage started to fall forward. He recoiled automatically, face contorted with horror and shock. The old man was dead . . .